Dear Mystery Reader:

All our lives we're encouraged to join up and be involved with our community. Americans are joiners. We clump together in groups, craving to be with our own. It started some time ago with the landing at Plymouth Rock, the first American foothold of the Puritan Pilgrim Society, if you will. However, if you read this book—or the other two excellent Graham Landrum whodunits: *The Famous DAR Murder Mystery* or *The Rotary Club Murder Mystery*—you might come to the conclusion that civic involvement can prove dangerous, even fatal.

My suggestion to you, gentle reader? Stay home. Read a good book.

You're holding one in your hands. The critics say so, and I agree. Said *Publishers Weekly* of this book, "Readers pining for a good old-fashioned mystery will find a splendid one here." I personally guarantee Graham Landrum's books are full of clever twists, wry repartee, and all the stuff you might reap from an evening out. However, there will be none of the danger, and you can stay in your pajamas. Read on.

Yours in crime,

Dana Edwin Isaacson
Senior Editor
St. Martin's DEAD LETTER Paperback Mysteries

Other titles from St. Martin's
Dead Letter Mysteries

THUNDEROUS APPLAUSE FOR GRAHAM LANDRUM'S MYSTERIES

The Sensational Music Club Mystery

"For a purely American cozy try Graham Landrum's *The Sensational Music Club Mystery*, the third in this charming series."

—*MLB [Mystery Lovers Bookstore] News*

"Harriet is delightful as she patiently rousts the skeletons from the closets."

—*Kirkus Reviews*

"Another down-to-earth look at small-town secrets."

—*Library Journal*

"Oh, how I love the ladies of Borderville, Tennessee!"

—*Meritorious Mysteries*

The Rotary Club Murder Mystery

"The 88-year-old widow again steals the show...a worthy colleague to Miss Marple. Charming and feisty as ever...in Harriet Bushrow the author has created an endearing woman...The locked-room puzzle is an added treat in this already delightful novel."

—*Clarion-Ledger* (Jackson, MS)

"Fans of locked-room puzzles will appreciate the inventive solution, skillfully demonstrated by Harriet at the scene of the crime."

—*Baltimore Sun*

(more...)

THE SENSATIONAL
MUSIC CLUB MYSTERY

GRAHAM LANDRUM

AS REPORTED BY
HARRIET GARDNER BUSHROW
AND HER FRIENDS

St. Martin's Paperbacks

THE SENSATIONAL MUSIC CLUB MYSTERY

Copyright © 1994 by Graham Landrum.

Library of Congress Catalog Card Number: 94-32377

ISBN: 0-312-96261-4

Printed in the United States of America

St. Martin's Press hardcover edition/December 1994
St. Martin's Paperbacks edition/July 1997

10 9 8 7 6 5 4 3 2 1

THE SENSATIONAL
MUSIC CLUB MYSTERY

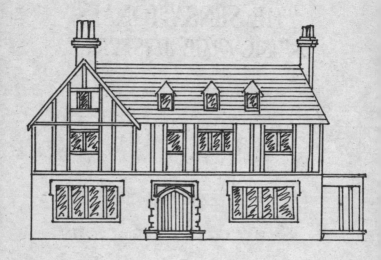

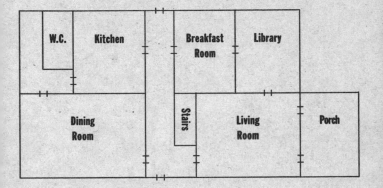

I

In Which a Dead Body Is Found
at First Presbyterian Church

VERA McKENDRY

First there was *The Famous DAR Murder Mystery*. Then came *The Rotary Club Murder Mystery*. And so when Monica Gaulton was found dead a few minutes before she was scheduled to participate in our annual Music Club Fashion Show, I suppose it was only natural that the press should refer to the case as "the sensational Music Club mystery."

Monica's death was beyond question sensational, inasmuch as it made headlines in *The American Exposé* and revealed a certain amount of scandal about one of our prominent families. In fact, there are still rumors and suppositions floating around town like a wind-blown virus—rumors about details and cover-ups. Consequently, it has been decided by all concerned to set out in a book exactly what happened and why it so occurred. In this way it is hoped that everyone's curiosity will be satisfied and we can forget the whole thing.

The first item to clear up is the role played by the Music Club, which in a way was only incidental, but was nevertheless very embarrassing—and especially mortifying to me because I had the misfortune to be president of the club when it happened.

The Music Club of Borderville, Virginia–Tennessee (our

1

town is divided by the state line), seeks to promote music in the lives of its members and in the community at large. We meet monthly except in the summer—with programs provided by our Music Club Chorus, our individual members who play or sing, and the pupils of those of us who teach. Of course we belong to the National Federation of Music Clubs.

We have fifty-six members. Six are men, and the rest of us are ladies—some teaching piano, violin, voice, and so on—but most of us are just individuals who studied music at some time and want to prop up our interest, so to speak, by promoting the love of music—'specially in our young people.

That is why we put on the Music Club Fashion Show each year—to raise money so we can award prizes to the elementary school, middle school, and high school students who win in our auditions, and scholarships to graduating high-school seniors for applied music instruction in college. Many who have taken music lessons in their early years go to a college or university to study business or pre-law and things like that. But if they have the encouragement of an applied music scholarship, they will go ahead and do something with their music in addition to studying those other things.

So we really go all out raising money each fall for our Music Scholarship Program. Then in the spring we always have the auditions and make the awards.

After we have written the checks for these grants, the money raised through the fashion show is gone. Of course club dues come in once a year, but that money is separate and barely covers dues to the Federation and the cost of our other activities. Except for the fashion show, we have no means of continuing our scholarship program. For many years now, the fashion show has been one of the social events of the season.

I suppose that in these days of women's lib, the idea of a fashion show is not only outdated but sexist. I can assure you, however, that the event is popular with the ladies in our town. Until last year, the tickets were not expensive. There was always a light luncheon—more like refreshments than a meal—and we had lovely table decorations with nice music. So a woman could reserve a table for eight or ten and pay off her social obligations, watch the show, help a young person with applied music at college or university, and just have a good time.

The Lea Ann Shop has always provided the fashions. Our members provided the food—sandwiches, salads, tea or coffee, etc.—all furnished gratis—and of course we had our members to provide the mistress of ceremonies, the models, and the music, and to sell tickets. It was always successful, and normally there would have been no reason for breaking the pattern. But last year two new features were added. And the combination of the two nearly wrecked the whole thing.

The first of these changes was suggested by Tolah Stalker.

Tolah is a very fine piano teacher—always has good students and pushes them forward as much as she can. In fact, she pushes everything she does—which is not a bad thing in itself, except that I didn't know how to deal with it.

Well, Tolah had this piano student—pretty girl—won everything in any competition she ever entered. She had an outstanding academic record too. But with that wonderful talent and all, the girl insisted she wanted to be a veterinarian.

Tolah simply could not abide the thought. Here was Tolah's big chance to see one of her students go on to be a concert artist. And, of course, our club was thrilled with the idea of contributing to a career like that. And when Tolah suggested that we change the format of our fashion show so as to bring in more money to provide a four-year scholarship for this young woman, the club went right along with her proposal. That is how our most recent fashion show became an elaborate catered luncheon with tickets at fifteen dollars apiece.

Believe me, that was a radical change. We all knew that the luncheon and the show would have to be good, or our name would be mud and we might as well give up the idea of success for the show in the following year.

In September, when we began making our arrangements for the show in October, everything seemed to be going fine. First Presbyterian Church, as it always did, gave us permission to use their fellowship hall, which was essential because it is the largest in town. Lea Ann, as usual, agreed to furnish the styles and the mannequins. Except for the new wrinkle of employing a caterer, everything was going as it had gone for so many years past.

Then came the big mistake.

I got this call from Ernestine Fuller, chairman of the Fashion Show Committee. Ernestine is a very willing person and just as sweet as can be. But she *does* judge people at face value.

Our conversation went something like this:

"Vera, I need to talk with you for a minute."

"About the show? How are things coming?"

"Oh, I'm just thrilled. I've had this wonderful idea. We could do the show a little differently this year and treat it as a cabaret."

I began to have a premonition. Ernestine is not an imaginative person. I felt certain that someone had been getting at her.

"A cabaret?" I said.

"Yes. I've talked it over with Lea Ann, and she thinks it is great, because it will be easier for her. She has so much to do getting the show organized with the models and the narration and all. Well, Monica Gaulton came into the shop one day last week, and she was talking with Lea Ann, and Lea Ann was saying how much work for her the fashion show is, when Monica said, 'Why don't you let me narrate the costumes for the models?' And Lea Ann liked that idea. So I called Monica, and we got to talking, and she had this wonderful idea of doing the whole thing as a cabaret."

This was a storm signal, and I knew it. I am afraid Ernestine had been taken in by Monica's claims of a career in New York and Las Vegas and other places. I began to see that Monica Gaulton was planning to take over our fashion show. .

For more than three years Monica has been a matter for speculation in Borderville. She was a native who went off to New York and those other places where she claimed to have been so successful. Now she had come back and married old Mr. Douglass Gaulton, who for some time had been expected momentarily to leave her a rich widow.

Opinions of Monica were divided. Those who had known the first Mrs. Gaulton were very cool to the second wife. But Monica had a certain following among newer people.

Ernestine herself had been the very one who proposed Monica for membership in the club and by doing so had ruffled the feathers of a good many of our ladies. Nevertheless we had admitted Monica. It would have been hard to turn down Mrs. Douglass Gaulton.

But to get back to the telephone conversation—

"Are you there?" Ernestine said when I failed to comment on Monica's proposal.

"Yes, go on," I said.

"Well, I called Lea Ann again, and she was delighted. She said it was just the thing. So we've been talking about it. Monica will accompany herself on the piano and just do the whole thing with songs from *The Fantasticks, The Three-*

5

penny Opera, and so on. It just sounds wonderful, and it will be so simple to do it that way!"

I did not know what to say. I hemmed and hawed a bit and said, "You mean that Monica is going to do it all! By herself! With nobody else on the program!"

"Oh yes," Ernestine assured me. "Monica has done all that sort of thing professionally, you know, and she says it will be no problem at all. And then, after the ladies have finished eating, Monica will describe the costumes while playing a little something on the piano. And she had this wonderful idea. She will introduce the different parts of the show with special numbers—like 'I Could Have Danced All Night' before she shows the formals—and . . ."

Ernestine bubbled on. It was obvious that the plans for the proposed extravaganza had gone quite far. Faced with that situation, I could not think of a way to put the brakes on without offending Ernestine.

But the other side of it flashed through my mind too. Monica Gaulton is by far the wealthiest member we have. Whether we wanted her in the club or not, we had her; and we didn't want to offend her in case we might need a contribution from her at some later date.

I didn't say yes to Ernestine's proposal, and I didn't say no. I said I would think about it and get back to her.

As soon as our call was over, I rang up Lea Ann. Somewhat to my dismay, she insisted that the new scheme was the only way to go. Monica had become one of her best customers. And, beyond question, Monica had a flair for clothes. I am told that Monica's mother was a dressmaker here some thirty years ago, which perhaps is why some people resent Monica's subsequent position.

What could I do? The club was totally dependent on Lea Ann for our styles. If this was what she wanted, I could hardly stand in her way even though I felt in my bones that the show would be in trouble. But I let Ernestine and Lea Ann—and, of course, Monica—do as they wished.

Well, that is how Monica Gaulton got to be the M.C. of our fashion show, and I can assure you that I was not the only person who was upset by it. But, undoubtedly, when the word got around, Monica's name helped us with ticket sales because people were curious. She had made such a to-do about being a professional singer, etc., that everyone was eager to see her perform.

So we had Monica as our featured entertainer, and we had sold a hundred seventy-three tickets at fifteen dollars apiece. On the morning of the show I was very nervous about how things would go.

I got to the church at ten-thirty. The caterer and her crew were hard at work setting up and decorating the tables. There had been a slight mix-up when the delivery boy at Don's House of Flowers took the geraniums to Second Presbyterian instead of First, but that all got cleared up. The people from Lea Ann's were bringing in racks of dresses and setting them up in various Sunday-school rooms.

The girls who were going to model the clothes began coming in, and poor Lea Ann was vigorously explaining how it was all to be done. I could see why she would think she had enough to do without having to narrate the show.

There was commotion everywhere, and it got worse as the time approached for our audience to arrive. I was sitting in the church parlor with a cup of coffee, hoping that everything would come out right after all, when Ernestine poked her head in and asked, "Has anyone seen Monica?"

I had. Monica had said she was going to get into her "costume." I supposed she was dressing in one of the classrooms.

Ernestine went off down the hall. I heard her cheerfully singing, "Monica! Monica! Where are you?"

There was the sound of the door opening and closing in the nearest classroom. But when the next door opened, Ernestine let out a scream that jerked me right out of my chair.

I ran to her immediately and was astounded at what I saw.

Monica Gaulton, wearing a man's full-dress suit, tails and all, was lying on her side on the floor. Next to her lay a flask, its cap having rolled some distance away. There was a battered, messy makeup kit on the nearby table.

Ernestine and I looked at each other in absolute shock. I don't know what Ernestine felt at that moment, but I passed from shock to fury. *This woman is drunk!* I thought. Then I noticed that Monica's eyes were open and there was no movement in them. The horror of it struck me like a thunderclap.

Just then Daphne Riggs appeared in the hall. Daphne is a doctor's wife and used to be a nurse. It was almost providential. I called to her.

"Daphne, we need you!"

Daphne came into the room and stood there in a matter-of-fact way. Then she stooped beside the body and felt first the wrist and then the neck. She snatched a tissue from the box beside the makeup kit and began to wipe the grease paint from Monica's face. She paused a moment.

"Look how pink the flesh is," she said. "She's been poisoned."

I heard Ernestine draw in a quick breath. As for me, I felt that the walls were falling and I was in the middle of the wreckage.

The reader will think I am dreadful, but all I could grasp was my own predicament. *I* was responsible for that fashion show—and the catered luncheon was supposed to begin in thirty minutes.

"Yes, she's dead." Daphne was very cool about it. "The pinkness is an indication of cyanide."

She picked up the flask, made of silver and covered with rather rough brown leather, and held it to her nose. Then she handed the thing to Ernestine.

"It is supposed to smell like bitter almonds," she said. "What do you think?"

Ernestine smelled of it and said she didn't know. Then she handed it to me.

I took the flask, and smelled it. I have no idea what bitter almonds are; but the odor I detected, beyond doubt, was whiskey. I handed the flask back to Ernestine, who held it to her nose again.

Someone said, "What is going on here?"

It was Helen Delaporte. She was standing in the doorway. Helen had been the president of the club the year before I was elected. She is one of those efficient people who always have things organized and know exactly what to do.

But I, at that point, certainly did *not* know what to do. Daphne was telling Helen that we had discovered Monica dead, and then I was telling Helen that our fashion show was ruined and I didn't see how we could possibly go on. A hundred and seventy-three women had paid fifteen dollars apiece for a luncheon and show that was supposed to begin in half an hour.

Difficulties kept crowding into my mind like waves, one after the other, all in confusion. How could we go on with the luncheon with a murdered woman practically in the next room? The police would be everywhere in a few minutes. And no matter what we all might have thought about Monica, she had been the wife of a leading citizen. What would people think if we went ahead with the luncheon with no regard at all to her death? Could we even *have* the fashion show without Monica? It struck me at once that only Monica knew what was to be said about each costume and when each number was going to be shown! And the more I thought about it the more I wanted to sink into the floor.

I must have been saying all these thoughts aloud, though I can't be sure of it. Anyhow, Helen understood, bless her!

She stepped to the table. A pair of slacks and a blouse were lying there as well as the leather coat that Monica had worn to the church. Helen rummaged under these and came up with a three-ring notebook.

"Ah!" she exclaimed as she opened it.

Thank God, Monica had typed out everything she was going to say for the show.

"Look," Helen said. "You three just go ahead and do exactly what you would have done if this hadn't happened. Have the custodian lock this door. We will not notify the police until after the show is over and all the women have gone. Meanwhile, as the ladies are eating, I will figure out something. Just go out there and be calm. Whatever you do, don't say a thing about this."

We all turned our eyes to that dreadful body sprawled on the floor, the silver screw-on cap, and the flask that the three of us had so thoroughly handled.

I remember when Helen Delaporte first came to Borderville and everyone immediately fell in love with her. Her husband was a young attorney just starting out, and they were the most attractive couple in town: he is from Louisiana, and she is a northern girl and such a gifted musician! And soon both of them were completely into everything here. They seemed to have been made just to live in Borderville.

Well if our show could be saved, I knew Helen would do it. So I did as I was told and left the rest to her.

It is hard to credit, but with Monica lying dead only a few steps away, the ladies in the dining room went merrily on with lunch, oblivious of the tragedy next door. But that was the way it had to be. If we canceled the show now, we would have to return fifteen dollars to each of the hundred seventy-three ladies who had tickets. And then there would be the caterer's bill for a hundred seventy-three lunches at five dollars apiece. I tried to figure it out in my head and realized that over eight hundred dollars would have to come out of our treasury and, consequently, there would be no money for scholarships in May.

Throughout the luncheon I could scarcely force a morsel down my throat. I am sure the ladies who spoke to me must have wondered what was the matter. Somehow I managed to eat a little, and it was time for the show to start.

Then Helen appeared at the piano. She began playing softly, increasing the volume until conversation ebbed away. We realized that she was playing "A Pretty Girl Is Like a Melody." Many of our members would be old enough to remember that.

We looked at the doorway through which the models were expected to come. And whom did we see but Harriet Bushrow?

Harriet is ninety years old—a certified grande dame if there ever was one—and the only one left in this town. There she stood—"posed" would be a better word—her cane at a jaunty angle.

She was wearing a gray wool suit and a brilliant orange silk blouse with, of course, her well-known cut-crystal necklace. Thrown over her shoulder was a tawny fox fur piece. She wore a gray felt hat, the crown banded with fur of the same color as the skins draping her shoulder. The brim of the hat was broad, and she turned to show her profile to the audience.

It was a stroke of theater that Monica could never have

matched. What I would have given to see Harriet Bushrow enter a ballroom in her youth! But perhaps she is better at it now than she was then.

Slowly she faced the audience and walked with great dignity to the lectern. Her gloved hand reached for the microphone and drew it to her.

"Good afternoon, ladies," she said. "No, I am not the pretty girl in the song. You ladies here"—she made a gesture to include us all—"are the pretty girls, and you deserve the stunning fashions we are about to show. I know we are all eager to see those beautiful things—things from the Lea Ann Shop that we will be wearing to Christmas parties, and the resort clothing for Fort Lauderdale and Fort Myers. And while we are dreaming—perhaps Bermuda or the Riviera. But first I must tell you that unfortunately our own little Monica Gaulton is prevented from being here."

She actually said that!

"And so," she continued, "I am afraid you will have to put up with me.

"And now to business—"

With that she opened Monica's notebook and read from it as though she had practiced the show for months. The models came out, strolled the length of the room, turning this way and that as models do. It was just perfect.

There was tremendous applause for every model, and Helen played on and on. I was overcome—overcome and grateful. The fashion show was going to be a decided success.

I won't report what the police said later on to Ernestine and Daphne and me when they found out how we had handled the flask from which Monica had drunk the poison. If we had not obliterated all interesting fingerprints, perhaps there would have been no mystery.

But what is done cannot be undone.

With this introduction, I'll let others take over the story.

II

A Few Things About Monica Gaulton

HELEN DELAPORTE

To be perfectly trite, Monica Gaulton could have been the original woman "of a certain age."

Of course those who knew her as a girl here in Borderville can tell you her age with precision. But when I first saw her, I was quite sure that she was older than I. She had dyed her hair that intense black that we see so often. But, on the other hand, she was so dramatic in everything she did that the black hair could well have been an expression of style rather than an indication of age.

And stylish she was. She wore that hair severely pulled back into a bun at the nape of her neck. Large, round earrings of red-enameled silver apparently made the desired statement about her personality. She normally used heavy makeup—but pale, to contrast with the hair and the earrings—much eye shadow and mascara. And I have to admit that the blue of her eyes was remarkable, although that perhaps resulted from the magic of contact lenses.

Whether one liked her or not, she was quite an item.

Not having grown up here, I saw her only as she was when she returned to our town about four years ago. She just appeared—without fanfare; but soon I was hearing snatches of conversation—"Have you seen Monica Taybrook?" "Did you know that Monica Taybrook is back?" Things like that.

For some time—to me at any rate—she was the invisible woman. All the old Bordervillians seemed to know of her presence. As for the rest of us—people who have moved here in the last thirty years or so—we had only heard of her. They said that Conrad Gaulton—he's the son of Douglass Gaulton, whom she later married—had shown an interest in her once and that the whole town had been pleased when the romance broke up and Monica decamped. It would seem that no one had heard from her during the years she was away. But now that she was back, she was decidedly a subject for discussion.

Then it became apparent that she was living in a duplex on Pecan Street near the park. If she circulated socially, there was no evidence of it. There was the inescapable impression that women who had known her—gone to school with her, at least—had no intention of "looking her up," as we say.

But her Pecan Street apartment was around the corner from Two-O-One Anderson Avenue.

Two-O-One Anderson Avenue was—and I suppose still is—one of the best addresses in Borderville. The house was built by the then-young Douglass Gaulton in the late 1920s. I am told that Douglass had just inherited Gaulton Office Furniture Manufacturing and Sales Co., as it was called then—it is Gaultwood now—one of our important industries.

The house, built for Gaulton's bride, is Tudor—the lower level being stone and the second story half-timbered. It has a high pitched slate roof with gables and many dormer windows. There are grand, tall chimneys and magnificent chimney pots that simply tower above the roof.

The Gaultons lived there as a "leading family" and raised a number of children—I think four—one dead and the others living elsewhere now. There is a grandson, who manages the business. Anyhow, when Henry and I came to town in 1961, old Mrs. Gaulton was certainly one of the social arbiters of the city, a gracious lady, extremely kind to me. She died about ten years ago, leaving Mr. Gaulton alone in that huge house, which must have seemed horribly empty to him.

People were always wondering why he did not go to one of his children or buy a condo. But he stayed on in the big house with a succession of attendants of one description or another. The Gaultons' black cook, who had been with them for so many years, had grown older and older; and although she never ceased to flutter like a mother hen about the various members of the Gaulton family, she did not have the strength to do what was needed to care for a man of Mr. Gaulton's age in a house of that size.

What I am getting around to is that about June or July three years ago, neighbors began to see Douglass Gaulton and Monica Taybrook sitting together on the porch at Two-O-One Anderson Avenue. Monica had become Mr. Gaulton's housekeeper.

"That won't last long!" was the general verdict. Some asked: "Do you suppose Jan hired her?" And the implication was that Jan had most certainly made a mistake.

Janet Gaulton is a granddaughter-in-law. She and her husband, Bill, live on Maple—about two blocks from the old gentleman.

It was soon known that Janet had *not* hired Monica. Mr. Gaulton himself had hired her. This fact created mild surprise. We had become accustomed to think of Douglass Gaulton as being "just a little past it." Not that he was really senile, of course, but he no longer drove his car; and more often than not, there was a little patch of silver stubble where he had missed a lick with his razor. He needed looking after; Janet supervised that until Monica appeared.

Monica Taybrook? People had thought Douglass Gaulton was pleased when Monica had left town—had perhaps even paid her to leave. And here she was keeping house for him!

Why?

Some thought Mr. Gaulton was tired of being controlled by Janet and was asserting himself by selecting his own housekeeper. After a few months, when it seemed to be working out pretty well, people began saying, "Jan ought to be relieved that the old man has Monica."

And so it went through that winter. Nobody saw much of Douglass Gaulton in those months. But when the weather was warm enough in May, Monica and her employer could be seen sitting side by side on their porch.

People smiled and said, "Much good will it do her!"

But late in June when Bill and Janet and their son, Nathan, got into their station wagon and headed toward the Grand Canyon and other points of interest, Monica loaded Mr. Gaulton into his Cadillac, headed for the city hall, and got a license.

Nobody knows the name of the minister or the witnesses. I suppose the family looked into it—for verification, if for no other reason. If so, they didn't mention it. Nevertheless the town soon heard of the wedding, for Monica immediately blossomed forth, appearing at numerous places in her new role, displaying a huge solitaire recognized to have been the property of the first Mrs. Gaulton along with a very showy gold band and announced everywhere that she was now Mrs. Douglass Gaulton.

There is a rumor that Bill, who is only a grandson even though he is in charge of the business, suggested that the marriage should be annulled. At which the old man is reported to have declared indignantly that annulment was now absolutely out of the question. It was also rumored that Bill didn't press the matter further because, although the old man was still chairman of the company in name, it was essential that Bill retain his grandfather's power of attorney in order to act for him in matters of business and run the factory.

All told, there was much ambivalence about Monica in this town where she grew up, from which she went away, and to which she returned some forty years later. The old Bordervillians united in snubbing her. The Taybrooks—at least the Taybrooks to whom Monica belonged—were considered to have been all right in their way. But Monica certainly did not come from a family that could aspire to a marriage with a Gaulton.

What, the establishment asked, had she been doing in those years she was away? They did not expect a reassuring answer.

Of course, Monica did not tell *them* directly, but she had much to say to others. She drove Douglass Gaulton to the country club for dinner several times—enough to establish her rights of membership as a Gaulton wife. Then she began to operate on her own. She played a little golf and was terrible at it. But in this way she was able to meet the "new" people. I have ceased to be "new"—at last—after thirty years. But a significant clutch of yuppies has landed on our shore in the last twenty years. Monica had considerable success with those people.

There is no doubt about the woman's sophistication. And the power of her personality was remarkable. She could move into a group having their drinks around the table at the club and within fifteen minutes be the center of attention. She called everyone by his first name—often without any introduction at all. It was not long before it was known everywhere—or at least said—that she had done something or other on the musical stage in New York.

On some people, this information, no matter how doubtful, acted as a magnet. Monica had become someone to know. But magnetism repels as well as attracts, and the old Bordervillians shook their heads and smirked.

I myself could not make up my mind. Apart from her undeniable style, there was nothing about Monica that attracted me. Too much brass, as far as I was concerned. But there had to be talent, too. And since none of us had ever seen her perform, it was possible that she might have enjoyed at least a minor career. Certainly from the distance of Borderville, it would have been easy for us to miss whatever glory she had achieved in the Big Apple.

I confess that I was among those who welcomed the occasion to see her perform as mistress of ceremonies for the fashion show. It was understood that she was going to sing (to her own accompaniment) as well as talk. Perhaps her taste would not meet the standards of our club. But there it was, and I could not criticize a performance I had not yet heard.

So when I went to the Presbyterian Church on that Saturday after Halloween—in retrospect, it was an appropriate date—I went with an open mind, expecting to enjoy, for whatever reason, whatever was to be presented. Then suddenly I found myself part of a bizarre drama when I saw Vera McKendry through that open doorway and got my first glimpse of a black-clad figure sprawled on the floor.

Poor Vera! She faced a catastrophe. If Monica's death became known, basic etiquette would demand that the show be called off. We would have to refund so much money; and then, if the police came immediately, there would be no way of hiding Monica's death from our audience.

And, of course, Vera could not be seen running about trying to save the pieces. That would give the secret away in no time. So without a notion in my head as to how I would do it, I heard myself say: "Don't worry. I'll figure out something. I'll take care of everything."

We closed the door on Monica and her death, and I searched out the Sunday School office. Fortunately there was nobody there. I sat down at a table and called Henry—that's my lawyer husband. After hearing the story, he agreed to make everything right with the police.

When that was done, I sat at that table for at least ten more minutes, trying to decide the best course of action. I had Monica's notebook, which was certainly a godsend. It contained very complete notes, perhaps provided by Lea Ann. And, of course, everything was written out in the order in which the ensembles would be shown. Anyone could get up and read from that notebook and the show would go off all right. But who? My brain was just paralyzed.

The Sunday School office at the Presbyterian Church is at the intersection of two halls. The door of the office opens to what may be called the front hall. Low cupboards line the rest of that wall and run all along the other side of the room. On the tops of the cupboards are stacks of devotional materials, etc. Then the walls above the cupboards, dividing as they do the office from the intersecting halls, are of glass and provide a clear view of both hallways. What I have called the front hall leads to a side door in one direction. And what I have called the side hall leads to a front door in another direction.

As I sat there waiting for inspiration, inspiration came into view.

Harriet Bushrow!

Readers familiar with *The Famous DAR Murder Mystery* and *The Rotary Club Murder Mystery* will understand my sense of relief.

At her advanced age, Harriet Bushrow has the liveliest brain and the strongest nerve of anyone I know. She is accustomed to managing the rest of the universe to suit her personal purposes with panache and éclat. If our country could elect a queen, we would have to elect Harriet, not as queen, but as queen mother.

I rapped on the window to attract her attention. Then, when the two of us were closeted in the office, I explained our predicament and told her what I wanted her to do.

She examined the notebook—made sounds of satisfaction—and said, "I suppose you don't want me to sing?" I thought for a moment that she was serious, but of course she wasn't.

She thought the situation over for about ten seconds. A mischievous light came into her eye as she said, "I'll do it."

She got up from the chair where she had been seated, hummed a bar or two, and took a few steps turning this way and that—like a model.

"But, Darling," she added, "when I come in, you must play this," and she sang a few lines of "A Pretty Girl Is Like a Melody."

III

DEATH OF SOCIETY WOMAN

The body of Mrs. Monica Taybrook Gaulton, 58, was found dead in a room in the Sunday School wing of First Presbyterian Church here yesterday. Stating first that the death resulted from mysterious circumstances, Police Chief Steve Roper expanded his finding to death by poison.

Clad in male evening attire, Gaulton's body was discovered by Ms.' Ernestine Fuller, 1709 Zolicoffer Circle, at 11:30 A.M. Saturday morning in the room normally used by the Gertrude Morrison Suggs Bible Class. Gaulton had been preparing to act as mistress of ceremonies at the yearly Music Club Fashion Show, which was about to take place only yards from the death scene.

Despite the sensational discovery nearby, the annual showing of women's styles proceeded as usual in the spacious dining room of the church. Over 150 women representing the cream of Borderville society chatted, cheerfully unaware of the nearby tragedy. "We were under obligation to those who had bought tickets," said Ms. Vera

McKendry, president of the Borderville Music Club, sponsors of the event. "We couldn't let them down."

Coroner Toberman cited cyanide as the poison employed. It is believed to have been administered in whiskey, a flask of which was found near the body.

Wife of Prominent Businessman

Mrs. Gaulton was the wife of Douglass B. Gaulton, president of Gaultwood, one of the pioneer industries of this city. Formerly known as the Gaulton Office Furniture Manufacturing and Sales Co., the industry was founded by the present owner's father, the late R. E. L. Gaulton.

The marriage of Douglass Gaulton to the former Monica Taybrook occurred three years ago. Since that time Mrs. Gaulton has become well known among the leaders of Borderville society.

Career Woman

Although born in Borderville, Mrs. Gaulton resided for thirty years in New York City. According to Ms. Edna Finch, proprietor of the Cup and Saucer Café and long-time friend of the murdered woman, Gaulton enjoyed an extensive dramatic and musical career under the name of Monica Tay.

IV

Of This and That

HARRIET GARDNER BUSHROW

When Helen Delaporte asked me to take Monica Tay-brook's place in the fashion show, I did not know what it would lead to. Helen is the one who got me mixed up in a murder mystery a few years ago. And the reputation I got for myself that time led to a second episode of a similar sort. Surely anyone would say that was enough for an old lady.

Yes, I was eighty-nine when that poor child was poisoned, but I have had a birthday since, and I have suddenly decided that I am old.

I don't know that I feel any different, and I have not been sick at all this past winter. But two more years? Three more years? If I don't start acting my age pretty soon, I won't have any time left to do so.

Of course at ninety I have aches and pains! I had aches and pains when I was a child, too. I am not going to let anything of that kind get me down now.

I walk with a cane, not because I have to, but because I know that if I should fall and break something, I might not get the parts back together just right. Besides, I have this gold-handled cane that was given to my grandfather Gardner by the Bar of Gloriosa County down in Georgia when he retired from the bench.* Engraved right on that beautiful gold handle it says: PRESENTED TO JUDGE AMOS HILLGREEN GARDNER BY HIS FRIENDS AT THE BAR, AUGUST 7, 1887.

Oh, I have a nice rubber tip on it so it won't slip or hurt the carpet or the floor.

No, I would say it is about time to give up mysteries and murders and things like that. But this mystery just seemed to be lying there waiting for me to come along.

To begin with, the reason Helen happened to see me in the hall was that I was late. I had misplaced the keys of my car and looked around for half an hour before I found them. I had put them in the Majolica vase where I keep my pennies. (Those pesky little buggers multiply like rabbits, and I never know how to get rid of them.)

So that put me at the right place for Helen to catch me just at the wrong time.

And then of course it was poor Monica that was dead. You see I was her Sunday School teacher back in 1946—or was it 1947? Anyhow it was right after Lamar and I moved back to Borderville. Lamar had been with the OPA during the war and had come back to be head accountant for the gas company.

Monica was unusual looking even then—and different from the other girls. It must have been hard on her. You see, the other girls did not like her. And I might as well admit that I didn't like her either.

I suppose a child psychologist would explain it as some kind of personality complex, and I can see how it happened myself, but that child was just downright mean.

Why, I have seen her for no reason at all stick a pin in the girl sitting next to her.

---

*In *The Famous DAR Murder Mystery*, Helen Delaporte said that Gloriosa is in South Carolina, but that sweet child is a Yankee and didn't know any better. She does now.

Monica's mother was Mosene Taybrook, a little widow. Her husband had been in the merchant marine during the war and was lost when his tanker was sunk way up there north of Norway somewhere. Goodness knows, the woman had a hard enough time.

Mosene was a first-rate seamstress—did beautiful handwork—made me one of the loveliest suits I ever had, just exquisite work. And the only thing she seemed to live for was that child.

With her mother pushing her all the time and the other children despising her, poor little Monica didn't belong anywhere. But she was certainly beautiful, and of course her mother made clothes for her that were prettier than any the other girls had. So I can understand why Monica was the way she was, even if I didn't like her.

When she first came back to town about four years ago, I didn't see her at all. But when she married Douglass Gaulton, there was nothing I could do but call on her.

Iris Gaulton—that was Doug's first wife—and I were very good friends—knew each other in the church, you know. And we were in the same little study club. And Lamar and Doug were golfing buddies and Rotarians together. So the Bushrows and the Gaultons saw quite a lot of each other.

But with Iris dead and Lamar gone, too—well, naturally, a widow doesn't call on a widower. But I always sent Doug a card on his birthday, and he sent me a pot of poinsettias every Christmas.

When I called on Monica, she was very cool about everything. I am sure she remembered I used to go to her mother's house for fittings, and she didn't like that a bit. She didn't know that Lamar had passed on; and after we got through talking about that, it was New York this and New York that; and I oh-ed and ah-ed and didn't let her get ahead of me one bit. Both of us knew there was a contest going on there.

I am pretty sure I would never have gone back into that house, but Doug had a stroke not long after he and Monica were married. The poor man is in pitiful shape—can't talk, can't control his limbs. They have to have nurses with him twenty-four hours a day, and you can imagine what that is like.

There is hardly anything that anybody can do for Doug. Still, he recognizes me, and tears come into his eyes when he sees me. But Janet, that's his grandson's wife, says that happens no matter who comes in. It is so sad to go over there, but I have done my duty. I try to see him once or twice a month. And now Monica is dead—and poisoned at that! With all that sensation, I felt bad for the whole family.

On the Sunday morning after they found Monica lying dead there on the carpet at the church—let me tell you, that Sunday was a show if I ever saw one!

The Gertrude Morrison Suggs Bible Class is the one I belong to—and that's the room where they found Monica. Well! The police had the room sealed, and there was that yellow tape that they put up around the "scene of the crime." So you can imagine what a sensation that was for all the old ladies in the class.

They had to put us in another room, and I believe the attendance was larger than it had been in months. The ladies in the class all knew Iris Gaulton—not socially, most of them, but knew her in the church. Iris was always very loyal to the church. Several of the ladies wanted to know if I was going to go to work and solve the crime.

I told them NO. I didn't have any idea of sticking my nose into anything like that. To tell the truth, considering the family and all the publicity, I just wished the whole thing would go away.

But, of course, in a town like this, a sensation of that size

26

would never go away, and I was just like everybody else, as excited as could be. All Sunday afternoon I thought about what had happened—couldn't get Monica off my mind. But I told myself that I was not going to put my paddle in the water this time.

For quite a while I have been working with the Borderville Literacy people. They do the most wonderful work of teaching people to read—grown people—some of them have even been to high school and can't read. When I was coming up, nobody ever got out of the first grade without knowing how to read. But that was then, and I don't know how we ever got to be the way we are now.

Anyhow, this literacy program is just the grandest thing. We use the Laubach method, developed by a missionary over in the islands. He drew pictures in the shapes of letters, and the students learn to pronounce them by the first letter of whatever the picture shows. It's a good, easy way to teach the sounds. But it still takes a teacher and a world of patience.

I am tutoring two people now. One is a man forty-eight years old. He's a janitor in one of the office buildings downtown and is just as nice and polite as he can be. I teach him at the Senior Center. But the other one—Mary Lizbeth—comes to the house.

She's a sweet little woman. She's a fry cook and dishwasher in a restaurant that is open just for breakfast and lunch, and so she comes by the house here for an hour twice a week after the restaurant closes.

The owner of that little café—it's called the Cup and Saucer—is Edna Finch, who was the one crony Monica had in high school.

So Edna had been talking, and Mary Lizbeth—that's my student—had overheard what she said, and Mary Lizbeth was just full of it.

Edna was saying that the police had been at her, asking

her all kinds of questions about the Gaulton family and how they got on with Monica.

Mary Lizbeth said Edna Finch as much as said the police thought one of the Gaultons had poisoned Monica so that Monica wouldn't get all of Doug's money when he died.

Now that is just awful! And then there was that story in the paper on the Monday after the fashion show and all that. I don't know why, but I cut it out, and here it is:

BANNER-DEMOCRAT   NOV. 9

POLICE QUESTION ABSENCE

OF GAULTON NURSE

Cause of Absence Unexplained

The investigation of the Gaulton murder took an unexpected turn yesterday when police learned that Ms. Dorothy Greene, nurse of Douglass Gaulton, husband of Monica Taybrook Gaulton, who was murdered last Saturday at the Presbyterian Church, was inexplicably relieved of duty between 8:00 and 10:00 A.M. on the day in question by Mrs. Gaulton. "I thought it strange myself," Greene told the *Banner-Democrat*. "It was not like her to take over any of the nursing. She called when I was just about to leave the house and said I shouldn't come until ten."

Police speculated that Mrs. Gaulton expected a private visit from the person or persons who may or may not have placed cyanide crystals in the whiskey flask from which Mrs. Gaulton later drank.

Flask Identified

Police Chief Steve Roper announced that the flask in question has now been identified as one owned by Douglass Gaulton, president of Gaultwood, Inc. Roper stated that between the hours of eight and ten there was no one in the Gaulton mansion other than the paralyzed Douglass Gaulton, Mrs. Gaulton, and the supposed visitor or visitors.

Nursing Routine

A team of three nurses is employed in the care of Douglass Gaulton, who suffered a near-fatal stroke two years ago. These care-givers are Ms. Greene, 3121 Culpepper, Borderville, Va., Ms. Teresa Thorpe, 1718 Polk St., Borderville, Tenn., and Ms. Alta Johnson of Piney Junction, Tenn. All three have been interviewed by police.

Does Motive Involve Money?

Questioned as to the motive for the murder, Roper replied that none had been determined at this time. He observed, however: "Where there is money, we can always find a motive."

V

The Day of the Funeral

HARRIET GARDNER BUSHROW

They had Monica's funeral on Wednesday morning in the chapel at First Presbyterian, and I went.

Poor Dr. McDavit was the minister. He didn't know a thing in the world about Monica, which was probably all to the good because he didn't have to lie about her.

He did very well with it. He imagined the joy with which her parents greeted her birth. Then he talked about her preparation for life when she was a schoolgirl. Then there was the bloom of youth. He got carried away on the subject of her career. He admitted that he did not know just what it was, but thought it was pretty good—or something to that effect. Then he mentioned how brief her happy marriage was. The moral of his remarks, if I am able to judge, was that we are here today and gone tomorrow. I suppose every preacher has a funeral service that he can pull out and use for somebody he doesn't know at all.

It was interesting to see who was there. Bill and Janet, of course, because they live here; and no matter how they felt about Monica, they would be the ones who would have to arrange the funeral and all that. And you would expect Virginia, too.

Virginia is divorced from her second husband, Mr. Pettitoe. Her first husband died. She lives in Knoxville, and it

30

would look very strange if she didn't show up for her step-mother's funeral, even though the stepmother was younger than Virginia. So that wasn't surprising.

But it *was* surprising to see Conrad and Norman there.

There were three Gaulton boys. The oldest was Bill. He's dead. The Bill that we have now was Big Bill's son.

Bill Gaulton—the father—was just the age of Lamar, Jr.; and they were very good friends when we were here in Borderville the first time—because, you know, Lamar, Sr., and I were in Washington for fourteen years—went there in 1932 with the New Deal and stayed there through the war. Big Bill's wife was Martha. She's married again and lives—somewhere. Anyhow, Bill and Martha had just the one son, and he's the only Gaulton in the third generation.

All right, so Bill was the oldest. Next came Virginia. She was about two years younger than Bill. Then came Conrad. He was born just before the crash in 1929. And Norman was born the first year we were in Washington.

Conrad lives in Oklahoma City. He is an engineer, and has something to do with oil-drilling equipment. He married a girl out there.

Norman is a CPA in Richmond.

Virginia, Conrad, Norman, Bill, Jr., Janet, and Nathan—that's Bill and Janet's boy—they were all at the funeral. But Virginia and the boys weren't in town exactly *for* the funeral. They were already in town. They were in town on Saturday, when Monica died. But that story comes in later.

I am sure the Gaultons had no tears for Monica. They were there just the same. Certain things have to be done for show, regardless of anything else.

Not counting myself and the Gaultons, there were about twenty-five people at the service. Four of them were from the Music Club. There were three Rotarians and one or two people from the church. The rest were people I didn't know—a good many of them right young, not yet thirty.

And some of them were dressed in a way you would not expect at a funeral. Monica's Country Club friends weren't much in evidence.

There was a little woman—rather heavy—with faded red hair. Her name is Edna Finch—the one who owns the Cup and Saucer Café, where my literacy student works.

And that was all the people who showed up. No neighbors, no old Bordervillians—not a whole lot of that crowd from the Country Club.

There was a good display of flowers.

I didn't go to the cemetery. They didn't bury Monica in the Gaulton lot in Rose Hill. They buried her next to her mother in Maple Grove. And I must say that was a clever way to avoid having to put Monica next to Iris Gaulton.

Everything was done properly, though the family didn't pretend to anything they didn't feel, and nobody can say they didn't do what was right.

Since the service was over by ten-thirty, it was a good time for me to look in on Doug, because, you see, the house is just a few blocks from the church. And it's hard to know exactly what to do in a case like that. I supposed Doug had a certain amount of real affection for Monica; and to leave him alone with just a nurse at the time of the funeral must have been melancholy for him.

So when the nurse—that little Mrs. Greene—came to the front door, she was delighted to see me.

"Oh, Mrs. Bushrow," she said. "Mr. Gaulton will be so glad to see you. He's been blue all morning."

"Then he knows?"

"Yes. We didn't tell him about the cyanide, but he knows the rest. There have been tears in his eyes ever since I came on duty."

Even though Doug's paralysis has left him completely helpless—has no control of his limbs to speak of, and can't talk but just makes a gurgling sound in his throat and tries so hard—you can tell he understands. I'm afraid it is just a living death for him.

As Mrs. Greene and I were going up the stairs, she said, "I think Mr. Gaulton had a premonition about Mrs. Gaulton. When I came in Saturday morning, he was awfully disturbed. The poor old thing kept trying to talk—tears just streaming down his face."

Because Doug does lots of crying anyhow, I thought Mrs. Greene was letting her imagination run away with her.

I said, "I saw Conrad and Norman and Virginia just now at the funeral. Are they staying here at the house?"

"Oh, no," Mrs. Greene answered rather quickly. Then realizing that her answer had been a little abrupt, she added, "They don't—well, didn't—get on very well with Mrs. Gaulton."

I let the matter drop.

It was pitiful when Doug recognized me. I leaned over him and took both his hands and told him he still had true friends. He made that noise in his throat. I thought I even felt a little pressure in his left hand.

I told him about the flowers at the funeral and named the Rotarians who had been there. But there's just so much and no more you can say to somebody who can't talk back.

I stayed a little while and chatted with Mrs. Greene. She told me all about her interview with the police. Said Monica had told her not to come until ten on Saturday morning but didn't tell her why.

When I got ready to leave, she came downstairs with me.

That house—and it's a big one—has a hall that runs straight through; and just inside the front door where the stairs go up to one side, on the right there is a large arch between the hall and the living room.

Now Iris Gaulton's people had always had plenty, and

Doug gave her money for anything her heart could desire. And that living room of hers was absolutely lovely. It wasn't just to my taste, but it was exquisite.

To begin with, Iris had a set of Belter furniture. You know what that is—rosewood with marvelous carving. It was her grandmother's—dates back to about 1850. I couldn't guess what it would bring today.

And of course Iris had everything that went with it—Persian rugs, coffee table, lamp tables and lamps—all antiques of the finest quality.

So of course I looked into the living room. Well, it was a shock to see. The only thing I could recognize was Iris's portrait over the mantel.

The beautiful Persian rug was gone and there was just a very brash kind of blue broadloom carpet. The furniture was new and cheap-looking. That place was more like a lounge than a living room—like something at a motel.

I said, "My goodness! What did Monica do to that living room?"

"Oh," said Mrs. Greene, "Mrs. Gaulton redecorated. The new furniture came in just a week ago.

"What did she do with the old furniture?" I was astounded that anyone would prefer that cheap stuff to the real thing.

"I don't know," the woman replied. "The movers came and took it out one morning. And when I came on duty the next day, the new furniture was already in."

It was perfectly clear that with Doug upstairs unable to move or speak, Monica had done all this on her own. I could imagine how Bill and Jan must have reacted when they found out about it. And I know Virginia must have had an absolute fit.

Mrs. Greene saw how I felt. She said, "I liked the old furniture better too."

"Oh," I said, "I knew the first Mrs. Gaulton—Iris—so

well. I can't tell you how many happy times I remember in this house. I know and love every stick of furniture she had. And all of it so like her sweet, sweet self.

"You know, I even remember the flask that they mentioned in the paper. Doug used to take it to football games. Oh, so many times Lamar and I went with him and Iris to the games down in Knoxville. And toward the end of the game when the wind would be so cold and the sun would be low and a shadow would come over our part of the stadium, I'd have a nip or two out of that flask."

I went on, "I remember that it used to be kept in the recess of that built-in cabinet in the breakfast room. I used to see it if I had a cup of coffee with Iris when I popped in of a morning."

"And that's where it was still," Mrs. Greene said, "ever since I have been here—that is, up until last Saturday."

"Oh, do you suppose it would be all right," I asked, "if I just peeked into the breakfast room?" I had something in mind, you see. "I haven't been in there since Iris died."

"Why certainly." Poor Mrs. Greene could hardly have said anything else.

Now, as I explained before, the hall goes straight through the house from front to back. In most houses the back door and the front door have different purposes—one for show and the other for service. But there is a drive behind the Gaulton house that goes from one side street to the other. And so the back entrance is the most convenient way to get into the house. That is why the back door was designed to be just as handsome as the front door. And certainly it was used as often.

I remembered all of this pretty well; but now that I knew the flask was still kept in the breakfast room, I wanted to get it clear in my mind how somebody could come into the house, fix up the poisoned whiskey, and pour it into that flask if that's what they did.

Whoever did it might have come to the back door, nipped into the house, done his or her work, and got out again in almost no time. It is such a big house that unless there were people in the kitchen or breakfast room, nobody would detect an intruder.

"That's what the police say," Mrs. Greene added after I told her what I was thinking.

I guess right then was when I knew I was going to work on this mystery the same way I worked on the DAR mystery and the Rotary Club mystery. I decided to look around as much as I could.

Now from the hall as you go to the back, the kitchen is to the left and the door to the breakfast room is opposite, to the right. Then there is a second door in the breakfast room. It leads to the library. Because there is another door that leads from the library to the living room, you can get to the breakfast room from the living room by going through the library.

The window of the breakfast room looks out to the back. Years ago there was a row of spruce pines along the back of the property. But they are all gone now.

"Oh, I just love these old houses," I said. "Such a gracious way of living!"

Now I'm going to interrupt my story and point out a few things about Monica's death that just seemed so obvious to me.

The poison—they said it was cyanide—couldn't possibly have been put into that flask while Monica was at the church. In the first place, who would go looking to doctor a flask of whiskey with cyanide at a Presbyterian church? And surely if Monica had left that Sunday School room for a minute or two, she wouldn't have left her whiskey out where anyone coming in could see it. And just as surely nobody could have poisoned that booze with Monica sitting there watching.

So there was no question but that the cyanide was in the flask before Monica left the house. And that meant that whoever poisoned the flask was in the breakfast room and would be somebody who was already in the house, or it was somebody who could come and go any time without being specially noticed. However you looked at it, the person had to know that the flask was kept on that recessed shelf in the built-in cabinet in the breakfast room.

Then there's another question: How would the poisoner know that Monica was going to take a flask of whiskey into the church? It is not something that is done very often.

I said to myself, "One thing at a time." If I could find out who was in the house between eight and ten on Saturday morning, I probably could figure out the rest from that.

So you see, it was my visit to the Gaultons' house that really got me into the mystery of Monica's death. And the more I thought about it, the more I just had to know how that cyanide got into Doug's flask.

Well, it was obvious that I needed some more information. Maybe something had been seen—somebody going in the back door or a car in the drive. And that made me think about the neighbors and what they might have observed. We are in the mountains here—Blue Ridge on one side and Clinch Mountains on the other. In between there is not much property that is level, and we have these hills all over town. So the Gaulton house sits on a fairly high terrace; and behind the property there is a pretty steep hill. Living at the top of that hill in a big old two-story home is my friend Olive Gifford.

Olive is about eighty-six and lives there with her unmarried daughter—a girl with a very responsible position in one of the banks. Olive has been badly crippled for years and can't get out of her wheelchair—an electrified thing that scoots around everywhere. They have a maid who stays in the house while the daughter is at work.

Olive has one of those chairlift contraptions that runs up and down beside the stairway. But because it is so hard to get her transferred from the wheelchair to this other thing, she mostly spends her days upstairs.

That sweet thing does all kinds of needlepoint and sits up there by the south window in her big lovely bedroom and just stitches and stitches. But that doesn't keep her from looking out the window, and I've never gone to see her that she hasn't told me stories about the neighborhood that make me think she keeps pretty close tabs on what people are doing.

Now I wondered: Wouldn't it be interesting if she had seen someone go into the Gaulton house on that Saturday morning? And since those trees at the back of the Gaulton property were gone, there was nothing to keep Olive from looking right down on the Gaultons' backyard.

So I drove up to the next street, parked my nice Buick that the Rotary boys got for me,* and paid Olive a visit.

The maid—an awfully nice little black woman—showed me up the stairs, and Olive seemed very glad to see me.

She had been doing needlepoint for some kneelers at the Episcopal church—such beautiful work!—a grapevine with leaves. I'm glad Presbyterians don't have such things, for I would never be able to do all that.

After I had inspected the needlepoint and admired it and had listened to what Olive had to say about her health, I said, "Well, what do you think about Monica Taybrook getting herself poisoned?"

Olive—she's just a mite of a thing—straightened herself up in her wheelchair. "She got what she deserved!"

I guess I wasn't expecting anything quite so strong. I said, "Oh, Olive, it surely couldn't have been that bad."

Olive sniffed. "Adventuress!"

---

*See *The Rotary Club Murder Mystery*.

I don't think I have heard that word since I was a girl.

"Now Olive, what makes you say that?"

"You wouldn't believe the strange things that go on at that house."

"Strange things?" I prompted. "What do you mean?"

"The kind of people that go through the door of that house are very different from the callers Iris used to have, let me tell you."

And then she did tell me. She said there was some group that seemed to meet once a month or more. And as Olive described it, the people were all young and came dressed as if they were going to a "tacky party." (Remember those?) She thought these young people acted very strangely.

"Always at night," Olive said in disgust. "And they sometimes made a ring in the backyard, and I can't for the life of me figure out what they were doing. Some kind of rite, I know. I heard them out there, and I could see them as clear as anything in the moonlight. I think it's this witchcraft we hear about nowadays."

"Wichcraft?" I said. "Surely not!"

"Well, the magazines tell us about that kind of thing. I spoke to our rector about it, and he laughed. But it made him nervous, all the same."

It was hard not to think that Olive was letting her imagination run away with her. At any rate, I hadn't come to hear about magic circles in the moonlight. I wanted to know what she had seen on Saturday morning between eight and ten. So I asked.

"Of course I saw something."

"And what's that?"

"A man." She closed her lips tight.

"What kind of man?"

"Workingclass man."

That's another expression my mother used to use.

"Workingclass man? Maybe he's a relative."

"I don't think so. The two of them didn't seem too pleased with each other. But she let him in."

"Monica let this man in?"

"Monica let him in."

"What did he look like?"

Well, she said he was about medium height and might be around sixty years old. Other than that, all I could get out of her was that he "looked like a possum."

"He drives up in an old blue car with one brown fender. Wears a cap with a bill."

So that was all the information I could get: medium height, middle age, wears cap with a bill, and drives an old blue car with one brown fender.

"Which fender was it?" I asked.

"One on the left in front."

"And was he here on Saturday?"

"Yes, he was."

What she had told me was all very interesting. There had been those young people that I had noticed at the funeral. Perhaps they were the ones who formed Olive's "Witch's Sabbath" in the moonlight. But I would never have suspected such behavior of them if Olive had not told me of it. I hadn't noticed anybody who looked "like a possum" at the funeral. And I had seen the cars in the parking lot, but none of them had a mismatched fender.

"Olive," I said, "I think your neighborhood has gone down quite a bit."

"You can take that for a certified fact!" she replied.

I stayed a little longer, and we talked about more pleasant things. When I see women like Olive, who can't get out of the house, I just wonder why the Lord has been so good to me.

VI

Inside the Gaulton Family

JANET GAULTON

Marriage brought me to a life very different from any I had known before. My father was a physicist, a university professor; and we had lived in places like Nashville, Berkeley, and Ann Arbor. I didn't know how it would be to live in a town like Borderville. I supposed there would be no shows, no symphony, no events of the sort I was accustomed to.

I was right about the last of these items. There are events, all right, but not the kind I knew before I came here.

Bill's grandmother was still alive then. I soon learned that Iris was the real force in the Gaulton family—quiet, persistent, intelligent. She was the balance wheel for Big Dad, as Bill called his grandfather. She kept us all on an even keel, doing it with so little effort.

And she was very kind to me. She showed me that a pleasant life was to be had in Borderville, Virginia-Tennessee.

But Iris was dying of cancer, and in two years she was gone.

Big Dad was lost without her. He had already turned the furniture plant over to Bill's father; and with Iris gone, he did not know what to do with himself. He grieved as only a dynamic man can grieve—for about nine months.

Then almost as if by magic he snapped out of it and was

doing very well when Bill, Sr., died. The second blow had much the same effect on Big Dad that the death of Iris had had.

Big Dad had been retired from management for almost eight years. During that time many changes had taken place at the factory; and when he went back, the frustrations were too much for him. Eventually he realized that he was no longer capable of carrying on the business. He retained his position as chairman of the board but stepped down from the management of the plant.

Gaultwood is owned by Gaulton, Inc., a family corporation. That meant that the board would have to select a new management, and the board consisted of Big Dad's remaining children and Bill, who had inherited his father's stock.

Big Dad wanted Conrad to come back to Borderville and take over the factory. But Conrad had become attached to life in Richmond and was not interested, as he said, in being the big frog in such a small pond. Norman was involved in manufacturing oil-drilling equipment and did not want to give it up. Virginia was recently widowed; so there was no son-in-law, and Virginia's education had vaguely to do with French literature.

That left my Bill to take over the management of the business.

Along with Gaultwood, we had the obligation of managing Big Dad, which at times proved to be more complex than running the factory.

He was by this time in his late seventies, living alone in that house, very insistent on having his own way, but unable to make things go. Fortunately, he doted on Bill, who is, if I may say it, a master politician. And equally fortunately, Big Dad has always been fond of me. But the member of our family who has had the most effect on Big Dad is our son Nathan.

When Nathan was small, Big Dad was still robust enough

to do things with him—treat him to the rides when the carnivals came to town, go with him to the park, buy him cotton candy. Big Dad spoiled Nathan terribly. And Nathan has always adored Big Dad.

Managing the house at Two-O-One was indirectly my responsibility. We begged Big Dad to leave that huge old place, but he refused. For sixty years he had eaten his dinner off that gleaming mahogany dining table, and he would eat it there until the day he died, he insisted.

That meant that he had to have a housekeeper. Have you recently tried to employ a housekeeper? If I were Kurt Vonnegut, I could write a book about the "housekeepers" we employed.

Actually, I couldn't blame Big Dad for firing most of them; but his reasons for dissatisfaction had little to do with their lack of general qualifications. As he approached what we could only call senility, he was harder than ever to manage.

That brings us to Monica.

One day she was simply there. Big Dad had fired Mrs. Sidlinger who had been in the position and put Monica Taybrook in her place. Neither Bill nor I had ever heard of her. She was poised, apparently capable, very presentable—and more important—she was a whiz at managing.

Having her with Big Dad was an immediate relief for me. It meant that I did not have to go to the house every day, inspect menus, see that the dust woollies had been removed from under the bed, haggle with the plumber when the toilet got stopped up—all those things that needed supervision.

So Bill and I rejoiced that Big Dad was in good hands and went off on our trip to the Grand Canyon, only to come back and find that Bill had a new grandma.

Things changed immediatcly. Monica had Big Dad completely in hand. We could never be sure whether he loved her or feared her. Whichever it was, the effect was the same.

The uncles and Virginia were furious. They had not liked it when Monica came into the house as housekeeper, but the marriage created a family explosion. It was obvious that they had experienced Monica before, though Bill and I did not know at that time what the experience had been.

But there was nothing any of us could do about it.

Fortunately, Bill had his grandfather's power of attorney. Since Monica did not know this at first, Bill was careful not to advertise it to her. Equally fortunate was the fact that Monica had shown no interest in running the company.

Then one Sunday afternoon, Big Dad suffered a massive stroke.

Ever since the marriage we had suspected that Monica had induced Big Dad to make a will in her favor. It was very difficult to suppose that she had not. And if she had, Big Dad's death would throw the family into major trouble.

The total number of shares in Gaultwood is 2,000. Of these, 1,020 were retained by Big Dad; 980 shares were held in Iris's name. When Iris died she left her shares equally to the four children. Since Bill had his father's stock, his interest equaled that of his uncles and Virginia.

What this means is that upon Big Dad's death the control of Gaultwood would be in the hands of Monica Taybrook Gaulton.

The family arrived here the day after Big Dad's stroke. We hovered around him in the hospital, wondering if the calamity would fall that day or the next. But the calamity remained suspended.

Big Dad could no longer speak or control his body. But he was still alive, though barely so.

The apprehension did not lessen; it simply lengthened into weeks, months, and now into two and a half years. The inevitable was nevertheless before us. Big Dad would leave us sooner rather than later, and Monica was poised for the event.

In the meantime, Bill, with his grandfather's power of attorney, had the upper hand as long as Big Dad lived. He took charge of his grandfather's income from Gaultwood and assorted investments. He provided Monica with what she needed, but no more. Monica was in an intolerable position; but Bill had recognized early on that Monica would have squandered everything if Big Dad's affairs had been left up to her.

Monica and I were at a complete impasse. We spoke to each other as little as possible. Though the nurses took their orders from Dr. McCallum, Monica continued in control as far as the affairs of the household were concerned. But we all knew that the equilibrium could not last long. Monica was crouched like a cat waiting for coming events, and we were all very uncomfortably aware of it.

We knew of Monica's shenanigans—the most outrageous ones. We knew she was gambling, but we did not know all the details, and she was not likely to confide in us.

That is pretty much the way it was when the corporation held its meeting on the weekend of the Saturday of Monica's death.

Virginia drove up from Knoxville Friday morning to stay with us. Norman flew in from Oklahoma City about midafternoon, and Conrad arrived by car from Richmond shortly before dinner. Since we have but the one guest room, the uncles elected to spend the night in the motel rather than in their stepmother's house, though, of course, they looked in on their father. For all it may have meant to the old man, his children truly did their share of hovering over his sickbed.

Shortly after lunch Virginia had gone over for a visit to Big Dad. When she returned to our house, she was livid.

"Did you know?" she demanded.

"Did I know what?"

"Did you know what she has done?"

"Why, no, Virginia. I have no idea what Monica has done."

"She has sold the living room furniture!"

That was an entirely new wrinkle in the situation. It had never occurred to Bill or to me that Monica would sell anything out of the house.

"That furniture came from the Ellison home-place and has been in the family for one hundred and forty years. It was to be mine. And that damned little bitch has sold it."

Virginia is a very mild-mannered person—very even-tempered—in fact, very kind. Rarely had I heard her so much as raise her voice. But now she was furious.

"Did you tell her it was yours?"

"I told her plenty." Virginia was walking up and down in our living room, her chin out, her arms folded in defiance.

"I had no idea," I said. "I hope you don't think I had anything to do with it or that Bill would have let it happen if he had known."

"Of course not," Virginia snapped. "Nobody could possibly predict what that piece of ---- would do," and she used a word I would never have expected of Aunt Virginia. But the normal mildness of her speech only emphasized the fury that now controlled her.

"Sit down," I said. "Let me get you a drink."

Virginia slumped into a chair and tapped her foot rapidly on the carpet.

As each of the uncles arrived, Virginia rehashed the indignity and very real loss that she had suffered. The uncles were less perturbed than Virginia; but they were not at all pleased.

Dinner at our house that night lacked the fun—the family stories and jokes—that we usually enjoyed at corporation meetings. After the meal and a few drinks, Virginia calmed down a bit; and things were almost on an even keel by the time the uncles departed for their motel.

The next morning, I would not say that Virginia was in a good mood at all, but she was at least pretty much herself.

As always, the corporation meeting was held in the conference room at the plant and would not take more than an hour or an hour and a half. That would give Virginia time to drive back to Knoxville before a late lunch. Bill would take Norman to the airport for his flight to Oklahoma City, and Conrad could easily drive back to Richmond by midnight.

Bill left the house about eight-thirty after having loaded Virginia's suitcase into her car, and Virginia left for the plant about ten minutes later. I did not see the uncles, as they had taken their breakfast at the motel.

Well, you know what happened that Saturday.

I had no intention of going to the Music Club's fashion show to watch Monica's antics. That would have been just too much.

I stripped the sheets from Virginia's bed and took them to the basement and then went grocery shopping. Aware that Monica would not be at home, I popped in to see Big Dad at about eleven-thirty. Mrs. Greene was on duty. She did not mention that Monica had connived to have her out of the house for two hours, and I really did not see anything unusual in Big Dad's condition. He always cries when I come in. It is rather touching, and I always felt ashamed that I came so rarely. But it was not the best idea to visit when Monica was there.

Bill and Nathan and I had lunch with Norman at the motel, and I came home in my car, while Bill stayed with his uncle until it was time to take Norman to the plane.

I was somewhat relieved. It was too bad about Virginia's furniture, but I felt sure she would live through the experience. My part of the Gaulton family could now relax.

But no.

The phone was ringing when I got to the house. It was the police, and the reader already knows what they had to tell me. I caught Uncle Norman at the motel before he and Bill could leave. And so Uncle Norman canceled his departure.

I called Virginia about three o'clock and gave her the news. I will not say that she was exultant, but I detected no regret in her voice. The police had the body, and the coroner was out of town. The autopsy was scheduled for Monday morning. So it seemed the funeral would have to be on Wednesday.

"Will you come?" I asked.

"Gladly!" Virginia answered.

Bill called Richmond and left a message on Conrad's answering machine. Conrad called us about eleven P.M. By that time, we had all realized that with Monica's death the threat to Gaultwood was over. If there was a will (and we were all sure there was one and that it left everything to Monica), it would mean nothing now. We were very much relieved and self-congratulatory.

Sunday was calm. We made no plans for the funeral until Conrad could return, which he did about eight on Sunday evening.

On Monday morning the uncles went to see Homer Sellwood, the mortician. Bill was at the plant when he got the call from the police. They wanted to interrogate each of us.

From the point of view of the police, we were the people most likely to wish that woman dead. And when *we* thought about it, we had to admit that each of us was very happy to have Monica out of the way.

Added to that was the fact that each of us could have had recent access not only to that flask but also to Monica's whiskey supply.

We were all under suspicion. Virginia had visited her father on Friday afternoon. She had been seen by the nurse, who had overheard her violent quarrel with Monica. But in that big house, there was no assurance that as Virginia let herself out, probably by the back door, she had not stepped undetected into the breakfast room, where the flask was kept. Virginia was very definitely a suspect.

As for Uncle Norman, Bill brought him in from the airport and checked him into the motel at about three-thirty. Then Bill brought him to our house, where he had a drink and was pretty much on his own until Conrad arrived at about five. We are only two blocks from Big Dad's house. It would have been no trick at all for Uncle Norman to saunter down to his father's, do a little business with the cyanide, and be back without our noticing his absence.

We all knew that before we had seen Conrad, he had gone by to look in on Big Dad. None of the family ever rang the bell before entering the house. After all, it was where they all grew up. And Conrad could have gone into the breakfast room on his way upstairs or on his way back without having attracted attention.

Then there was Bill. He left our house at eight-thirty on Saturday morning. And as the police discovered, Mrs. Greene did not come on duty until ten. Bill had as much opportunity as anyone else. Moreover, because of Bill's position in the company, he stood to lose more than anyone else if Monica inherited Big Dad's Gaultwood stock. The police point of view was that Bill easily could be the culprit.

And what about me? I was in that house more than any of the rest of them. And Monica and I generally avoided each other. The insidious thing about poison is that it can be placed where it will be taken later—maybe a few hours, maybe weeks.

It isn't at all surprising that the police would view the Gaulton heirs with marked interest.

And so they started with Bill—probably because he was the easiest to locate.

They asked him about his movements during the three

days preceding that Saturday. He gave them as good an explanation as he could.

Then they wanted to know if he had ever expected to inherit from his grandfather's estate. He said he had once understood as much.

Did he know that his grandfather had made a will in favor of his second wife? They had found it, you see.

Bill was very frank. He said he had assumed that such was the case.

Then it came out that Bill had held the purse strings for his grandfather and that Monica had to be kept in check financially.

Bill admitted that there had been acrimony, but that had climaxed about two weeks after Big Dad's stroke. Bill thought that Monica had given in at that time because she did not expect Big Dad to live longer than a week or two. And, no, Bill had seen no evidence that Big Dad's death was immediately imminent.

Bill came home from the interrogation and said that he had passed Uncle Conrad in the hall at the station and supposed that the police were with him then.

We had had our lunch and were all sitting in our living room—Bill, Uncle Norman, Virginia, and I—when the police drove up with Uncle Conrad and then took Uncle Norman away with them.

I had saved some chicken salad from lunch and made a peanut butter and jelly sandwich, which I served to Uncle Conrad with a cup of cappuccino—powdered, I am afraid—on a tray in the living room. We all wanted to know what had taken so long.

"They wanted to know all about 1952," he said.

" 'Fifty-two!" Virginia exclaimed.

"Yes."

"What about 1952?" Bill wanted to know.

"That was the summer Monica worked in the office at Gaultwood," Conrad replied.

"Monica? Worked at Gaultwood?" Bill was incredulous. Neither he nor I had ever heard of it. It seemed hardly possible that we had not.

"Yes," Conrad went on. "It was Mother's idea. She had her dresses made by Mrs. Taybrook and thought very highly of the woman because she was a good seamstress who was poor and worked very hard. Mother was always helping somebody. So she persuaded Dad to take Monica on as a substitute for Miss Brumbaugh, who was recovering from an operation."

Virginia cleared her throat in an icy sort of way. She had her arms folded as they had been during her tirade against Monica on the Friday before.

"I may as well tell you," Conrad confessed. "The police have found out that I got Monica pregnant that summer."

Bill and I could not have been more shocked if we had learned that Margaret Thatcher had become a Socialist.

But our amazement was nothing to Virginia's reaction.

"You and Monica!"

"I am afraid so."

"Nothing of the kind."

Conrad smiled a guilty smile. "I guess I ought to know."

"Oh, you fool," she said. It wasn't you. It was Norman."

Now it was Conrad's turn to be surprised. As for Bill and me, we might as well not have been in the room. The brother and sister had forgotten about us.

"Norman? What are you talking about? And what do you know about it anyway? Nobody knew about it—nobody."

"I tell you it was Norman. That poor boy. He couldn't go to Dad and he couldn't go to Mother. So he came to me. And Monica—that slut! She was a full two years older than Norman anyway. She engineered it all—got her fangs into him and wouldn't let go. Oh no. 'He had ruined her!' How quaint! You can't ruin a woman like that."

"Virginia, Virginia," Conrad protested. "You have it wrong."

"Wrong? I pawned my gold bracelet with the sapphires and diamonds that Dad gave me on my twenty-first birthday to help Norman pay her."

Conrad was astounded. "But I paid her—paid her two hundred a month to go off and have the baby. She went to a place in Roanoke until the baby came, and then she put it up for adoption."

"You fool!"

"Yes, I know."

"You *and* Norman. There is more excuse for Norman, but the both of you let that bitch make fools of you. And the worst of it is that she made a fool of me, too."

Well there it was. It appeared that Monica had put herself in a position to accuse both Conrad and Norman of paternity. And she had calmly collected from both. Then—according to Conrad—she had kept the baby with her in New York for a year before she put it up for adoption.

Conrad said he had a picture of the baby—it was a boy.

That was it—the family scandal in the open. When the police delivered Norman to the house, Virginia immediately lit into him. He too had paid Monica two hundred dollars a month. Fortunately, he had had a generous allowance; but even with Virginia's help, it had been very difficult, for Norman had been in his first year of college when it happened.

The revelation only renewed Virginia's anger over Iris's living room furniture, and I am afraid her animus toward Monica was very evident when the police questioned her on Tuesday.

That old secret, not fully shared by the three siblings, went far to explain their reaction when Monica had become their father's housekeeper. They showed their disapproval, but they could not interfere. Monica held the ace. She could tell her story. And although the story was very old, none of the three wanted it known.

Imagine their dismay when Monica married their father. Regardless of the openness about sex that has developed in the meantime, it must give a son a queasy feeling when his father marries the son's former mistress. There is just something slimy about it. And in the Gaulton family!

The police interrogated Virginia on Tuesday morning. When she returned to our house, she was glum, but she had herself under control.

Then in the afternoon it was my turn. The police were friendly, and I answered their questions as frankly and openly as I could. They seemed to accept my statements.

They asked me many questions about what I knew of Monica's relations with Virginia and the uncles. I did not like this at all. I was glad that I could honestly say there had been no violent, open hostility except for the incident of the living room furniture. Surely they would not think a thing like that would goad Virginia to the crime of murder. But I was not at all sure that the police were of my mind.

And, oh yes. They had asked Virginia if she had known that her brother had fathered a child by Monica Taybrook. Virginia had had to admit the truth—the whole truth, I'm afraid—about Norman as well as Conrad.

At this point the reader probably thinks I should close this chapter. But our surprises are not over yet.

The Gaulton family was on a roller coaster of sensations. Friday, Saturday, Sunday, Monday, Tuesday, and Wednesday—one strange day seemed to follow another.

Tuesday was taken up with, of all things, visits of condolence. And then there was the problem of Mr. Sellwood, the undertaker, who insisted on being sympathetic. He had pressed so for a "viewing" that at last we had acquiesced, but we insisted that the casket must be closed at the church. And then there were all those flowers. From business associates, fraternal orders, and that sort of thing; but also from people who were too embarrassed to know what else to do. And all of those sprays would have to be acknowledged.

Wednesday was the funeral. The attendance was very small, which was just as well for us, because we felt perfectly hypocritical sitting there in the front row for the funeral of a person who to us was the very epitome of the wicked stepmother. Besides, it was in the mind of each of us that if the police suspected us of murder, there would be others who had leapt to the same conclusion.

We got through it and came home feeling relieved. We were sitting around having drinks when the phone rang and we received yet another surprise.

Bill, who had taken the call in the kitchen, came into the living room and said, "Uncle Conrad, it is the police again. They want to talk to you."

The room became silent as as we strained to hear what Conrad was saying in the kitchen.

It went:

"Yes—

"And what did it say?

"Are you sure?

"While I must say that I am astounded, I am glad to hear it. And thank you so much for telling me."

Uncle Conrad came back into the living room, saying, "That was considerate of Sergeant Gallager."

Sergeant Gallager is what passes for the detective on the Borderville police force.

"What was?" Virginia demanded.

"Well he says"—Conrad looked at his brother with half a smirk—"he says that the coroner's report indicates that Monica never had a baby at all."

But the damage was done. Conrad and Norman had *thought* they were the fathers of Monica's child. And as far as motive was concerned, their belief in their paternity would involve them in suspicion—suspicion about what? Well, at the least the brothers had been blackmailed.

VII

At the Cup and Saucer Café

HARRIET GARDNER BUSHROW

After my conversation with Olive on the Wednesday of th
funeral, I went home and thought about what she had said
I wondered if the police knew about the car with one brow
fender or about the figures Olive had seen from her win
dow—or thought she had seen—standing in a circle in th
moonlight.

If they didn't know, perhaps I ought to tell them. Bu
then I remembered how the sheriff had reacted in the DAF
murder mystery when Helen Delaporte tried to tell him
what we knew about the dead man we found at the Brow
Spring Cemetery. He thought we were just old women with
imaginations that were working overtime.

Since then, I have had a little triumph over the Virginia
police in clearing up the Rotary Club murder. But in the
present case, I was not the one who had actually seen the
man go through the Gaulton's back door, and I had not
seen those people out there in the moonlight. Would the
police take Olive seriously? If you put a report of a car with
one brown fender together with a report of people dancing
in the moonlight, it sounds mighty peculiar.

Whether the police believed her or not, I was sure that
Olive had seen something, that she was probably right and
that it was in fact mighty peculiar.

I finally made up my mind. It was up to the police to talk to Olive if that was their desire. The police could see as well as I did that Olive's house is on the hill behind the Gaulton place. If I could figure out that she might have seen something, they could figure it out too.

Now why did I get a bee in my bonnet about this thing with Monica Gaulton?

It is hard to explain. When you get older, you think of your own life and ask yourself if you have ever done anything worthwhile. Maybe you find a little something that you can be proud of. But that is all in the past, and most of the people who knew about it are dead anyhow. Then you think: Is there anything important I can do now, because there are not many years left. Most people, when they get to thinking in this way, say: I'm going to write my memoirs for my family, or I'm going to label all my keepsakes so the children will know the importance of each one, or something like that.

I remember when I was at Catawba Hall Miss Langrock had me memorize a poem that went:

> You and I are old;
> Old age hath yet his honor and his toil.
> Death closes all: but something ere the end,
> Some work of noble note, may yet be done,
> Not unbecoming men that strove with gods.

I didn't understand it then; but, oh, I do now.

So you might say I was just itching to get at this Monica Gaulton murder; and the man with the brown fender and the figures there in the moonlight dancing around were my own private clues, and I would just keep them that way—at least for the time being.

Well, the funeral and my visit to Doug Gaulton and to Olive were on Wednesday. Thursday at five Mary Lizbeth

57

came for her literacy lesson—she comes Mondays and Thursdays.

We had our lesson, all right; but we had a nice little conversation.

"Mary Lizbeth," I said, "I suppose they are still talking down there at the Cup and Saucer about this Monica Gaulton thing."

"Oh, yes. Everybody that comes in—'cause, you know, Monica was working down there a little while before she went to keep house for Mr. Gaulton."

Now that was something that I did not know.

"She was?"

"Lord, yes. When she come to town, she didn't have much more than the clothes on her back. Why she was pore as me. And just look, she went and married that Mr. Gaulton. But it never done her any good in the end."

Now there's philosophy for you.

"And she worked at the Cup and Saucer? I bet she didn't like the work."

Mary Lizbeth laughed. "Not hardly," she said.

"How was she to get along with?"

"Never paid much mind to me. 'Course she was in the front, and I was in the back. And I wasn't nobody for her to notice anyways."

"What do you mean?" I demanded. I have a lot of respect for Mary Lizbeth, and I didn't like it that a dressmaker's daughter looked down on a fry cook—though I suppose we are all snobs. What we see and how we see it depends on where we stand.

"Oh, Miz Bushrow, how could she think anything of me? She was so beautiful and, you know, classy."

"And mean and hard to get along with," I added. I explained how Monica was in my Sunday School class and stuck the pin in that girl.

Mary Lizbeth seemed not to resent Monica's slights to

herself, but she did not like it that Monica wasn't nice to Edna—that's Edna Finch, the woman who runs the Cup and Saucer—the friend that Monica went to when she first came back to town.

"How do you mean, not nice?" I demanded.

"Oh, it was like all the shows and such she had been in in New York, and the famous people she saw out in Vegas, and when she used to have money, and just anything like that. And the rest of us just weren't nothing."

But apparently Edna had not resented Monica's airs. I suppose she got a little reflected glory out of a friend who could toss stories like that around.

"Mary Lizbeth," I said, "do you think that if I were to go down to the Cup and Saucer sometime, Mrs. Finch would have time to talk to me about Monica—you know, seeing that we both knew her and that sort of thing?"

"Oh yes."

Since the Cup and Saucer is downtown, where there is only a clientele of office workers, the café closes at four. Mary Lizbeth says shoppers and lawyers come in for a coffee break in the afternoon, but after three-thirty there is hardly anybody in the shop.

I decided that I would do some shopping on Friday afternoon and just accidentally stop in at the Cup and Saucer a little before closing time.

The Cup and Saucer Café is on Seventh Street, half a block from Division.

Seventh is a narrow street, and the buildings are old—older than I am, and just about as shabby.

Well, the Cup and Saucer Café is on the ground floor of a grimy, red brick building—three stories tall with the old-fashioned zinc cornice that all buildings used to have. No paint on the cornice—upstairs windows covered with dirt—upstairs empty. I wouldn't be surprised if the Fire Marshal told them they couldn't rent the upstairs.

But the windows of the café itself were clean and bright. I expect cleaning them is one of Mary Lizbeth's jobs.

The sign hanging over the sidewalk says CUP AND SAUCER CAFÉ and shows a big picture of a cup and saucer.

Menus are stuck inside the front window for people to read from the outside.

When I closed the door behind me, the woman at the cash register looked up from her magazine. It was Mrs. Finch. There were not more than two or three other people in the room.

"Good afternoon," I said as I heaved myself onto the stool at the counter. It was the closest stool to where the woman was sitting. "I'd like a cup of coffee, please."

The woman got up and poured very black coffee from one of those round glass jugs that they keep on those hot plate things.

"Cream?"

"Oh, yes, please."

She put the little plastic cup of half-and-half on the side of the saucer and placed my coffee on the counter in front of me.

"That will be fifty cents."

"It's getting chilly out there," I said as I got my coin purse out of my pocketbook. "I'm afraid winter is going to be early this year. Aren't you Edna Finch?"

"Yes."

"I'm Harriet Bushrow. I believe my little pupil works for you. Mary Lizbeth Sykes. She has told me so much about you."

Edna Finch warmed up to me immediately. "Mary Lizbeth says you knew Monica Taybrook," she said.

"Yes indeed. I knew her, and I knew her little mother. What a terrible thing to happen to that beautiful girl!"

"Tragic! Just tragic!" Edna Finch is a little on the plump side. I would say she is about five foot two. She was not wearing a waitress's uniform, because, of course, she is the owner. And so she had on a sweet little nylon dress, blue with a figure of large gray lilies. Close up, there was more gray in her red hair than I had observed when I saw her at the funeral. After all, she was the same age as Monica.

"Yes, it was tragic. Mary Lizbeth says Monica worked here in the restaurant."

"That's right. She worked here until she went to work for Mr. Gaulton."

"Well, well. And you and she were friends before she went off to her glamorous career in New York."

"Yes."

"That was a long time ago. I suppose you kept up with her all that time?"

"Yes—well, not exactly. You know how those things are."

"Yes indeed," I said. "We are so faithful to write for a year or two, and then maybe we exchange cards at Christmas until one year it doesn't happen and we pretty well lose track of our friends. But you *did* know all about her career. They mentioned it in the paper. I suppose that must have come from you."

"Yes, the reporter was in here. You probably noticed, she mentioned me and the Cup and Saucer in the story."

"Yes, I noticed. And I imagine you might have something to tell the police about who could have put that poison—such an awful thing—in her drink, whiskey, they said. Tell me, did she drink quite a lot?"

"No—no, I wouldn't say that. She might have a little beer now and then. And she liked vodka. But she didn't do much drinking."

"Then how do you suppose the one who did it would think to put it in whiskey if it wasn't something that Monica was likely to want?"

"Well now, she might have grown a taste for whiskey

after she went to work at Gaulton's. She told me that she and old man Gaulton had Old Granddad on the rocks every afternoon before suppertime. But while she was staying with me she didn't have any Old Granddad. I don't have the money to have liquor all the time, and of course we don't have a license here."

"I suppose the police asked you about that—I mean about Monica's drinking habits. They did talk to you about her, didn't they?"

"Oh yes, they asked me about a hundred questions, but they didn't ask me what she liked to drink."

"Is that so? Well, I wonder just what they would ask if they didn't ask about that."

You see, I wanted to get her to open up and just talk to me, and I was lucky to have asked a question that the police didn't think of, because that did the trick.

She told me all about how Monica simply showed up on her doorstep one day about four years ago. Edna recognized her, all right, but she was very much surprised when she realized that Monica was moving in.

Edna said she didn't have a spare room in her apartment, and so Monica had to sleep on the sofa bed in the sitting room.

Monica had a car and a gas card with somebody else's name on it. She said a man in Las Vegas had told her to use it until she could get another "singing engagement." And that was about all she had except for a few dollars in her purse.

She asked Edna if she could stay for a few days. When the few days turned into three weeks, Edna suggested firmly that perhaps Monica would help her out at the Cup and Saucer.

At breakfast and at lunch it takes two waitresses to handle the Cup and Saucer customers, and one of them had left without notice just at that time. So there was a real need for Monica in the café.

"I bet most of your customers are men," I said with a kind of suggestive look out of the corner of my eye. "How did Monica like that?"

"I tell you the truth, Mrs. Bushrow, she put the make on every man she waited on. Got good tips too."

"Was there any one particular man that you can think of?"

That must have been another question that the police did not ask.

Edna thought it over and said, No, there wasn't any one man that seemed to take to Monica. But now that she thought about it, there was one strange thing.

"It was just before Monica quit working here. About one-thirty, when business had pretty well slowed down, a man I never saw before came in and sat just about where you are now. Monica was in the kitchen picking up an order. I just happened to be looking in her direction when she came through the door and saw the man at the counter.

"You would have thought he was a spook. She just froze about as long as it would take to count to ten. Then she turned around and went back into the kitchen. She gave the order to the other girl that was working here then. She didn't come out of the kitchen until the man left."

A week later Monica had sold her car and moved out of Edna's place into an apartment near Doug Gaulton's house. She quit working at the Cup and Saucer and became Doug's housekeeper.

All of this had happened two months or more after Monica showed up at Edna's place with a borrowed gas card and almost no money.

I wondered if the man whom Monica wanted to avoid might have impressed Olive as looking like a possum. But that description is not very precise. I told Edna that she had a lovely little restaurant, and that I was going to come back now that I knew about it.

Then I made a detour into the back of the shop to say hello to Mary Lizbeth and went home.

There it was—definitely a mystery man—someone Monica did not want to see. That much of what Olive had told me was accurate. Next I thought I would look into those people playing ring-around-the-rosy by moonlight in Doug's backyard.

VIII

Harriet's Birthday

HELEN DELAPORTE

What grander occasion can there be than the celebration of the ninetieth birthday of someone who is still hale and hearty—a celebrant who still does all the things he/she has always enjoyed?—well, almost all!

The nonagenarian of the moment was, of course, Mrs. L. Q. C. Lamar Bushrow—our own Harriet. Born in Georgia of a well-established family, Harriet married Lamar Bushrow, distant cousin and namesake of the late Supreme Court Justice Lucius Quintus Cincinnatus Lamar. Harriet and Lamar made Borderville (Tennessee side) their home shortly after their marriage in 1919 and remained here until Mr. Bushrow, who had lost his business in 1930, was employed in Washington by a New Deal agency. During World War II, Mr. Bushrow served in the OPA.

After the war the Bushrows returned to Borderville, he to work for the gas company, and she—well!—she to activate the town.

Harriet has held the locally highest offices in the DAR, the UDC, the YWCA, the Presbyterian Woman, Altrusa, the Woman's History Club, and the Borderville Antique Club. She has recently been invited to join Pen Women.

It was Harriet who cleared up the famous DAR murder

65

mystery when I was regent of the Old Orchard Fort Chapter. And it was Harriet who explained the Rotary Club mystery. My Rotarian husband, Henry, and I feel a special obligation to Harriet Bushrow, and affection, not only because of her unusual contribution to our respective organizations, but more particularly because of her charm, intelligence, and old-fashioned courage.

One morning at the breakfast table, Henry looked up from his paper and said, "This is the eighth of November."

"I know it is."

"A couple of days ago you said Mrs. Bushrow has a birthday in this month."

"On the eleventh."

"What are we doing about it?"

"We are taking her to dinner at Ted's."

Ted and Betty Kyrides run the excellent Greek restaurant here in Borderville.

Henry put his nose back into the *Banner-Democrat* and didn't think about Harriet's birthday until I reminded him of it on the eleventh.

At six-thirty we picked up Harriet at her modest home and arrived with her at Ted's by seven. After Harriet had removed her coat and I had hung it up, Henry opened the florist's carton he had been carrying and pinned a white orchid on Harriet's shoulder.

She dropped a curtsy and, lowering her eyelids in mock bashfulness, said, "You are most gracious, kind sir," and beamed like the rising sun.

Our table was reserved. Betty Kyrides herself brought us the menus. We had the option of American, Greek, or seafood entrees. Harriet chose the Greek—dolmathes. Henry ordered a bottle of white wine, and we toasted Harriet.

She proposed the following as a counter-toast:

66

Here's to the years of the future,
So long as life shall last.
Here's to the joys of the present
And no regrets for the past.

When the agvalemono soup was served, we lapped it up for a minute or two before Harriet broke the silence.

"Mr. Delaporte, do you hear anything about the progress of the police in solving our most recent murder?"

"Why, yes, Mrs. Bushrow. It seems that the late Mrs. Gaulton had quite an interesting career before she favored our community once more with her presence."

"I don't doubt it," was Harriet's crisp comment.

"She came here from Las Vegas, you know."

"So I have heard."

"She is said to have been performing out there."

"Singing for her dinner?"

"Yes, but also losing large sums."

"Large sums! I would expect that of Monica. She would never lose just a little. She would always lose a lot. What a strange girl!—when you think of her modest little mother. How do you suppose she got those 'large sums' to lose in the first place?"

"That, I suppose, is another mystery."

"Tell me, Mr. Delaporte, could the loss of 'large sums' have led to Monica Gaulton's murder?"

"Mrs. Bushrow," Henry said, "I do not know that it did, but there is always the fact that Vegas is a prime base of the Mafia. It is possible that her death was connected with the mob somehow."

"But, Mr. Delaporte," Harriet objected, "Tennessee is a long way from Las Vegas. Could our little Monica upset those criminals so much that they would come all this distance to kill the poor child? Don't you think that is a little farfetched?"

"I would suppose the police have information to support their suspicions." Henry replied, "The Mafia is like any of the major business conglomerates. It is not confined to Las Vegas or New York. Those people invest their capital in many ways. No doubt the Mafia has a presence even in Tennessee and Virginia."

"Gambling is illegal in Tennessee, isn't it?" I asked. I suppose it was a foolish question; but with the changes I have seen in American mores, I really didn't know.

Henry launched into a lecture on anti-gaming laws in general. It seems that as a nation we do not know what we think about gambling. Is it a sin, or is it a folly? Is it forbidden because by gambling one harms another person? Or do the laws aim at protecting the individual from himself? Now that common wisdom says that a citizen has a right to destroy himself entirely through suicide, may he not destroy himself economically through gambling?

But then there is the social atmosphere of gambling that seems to be both a moral and an economic pollutant. Gambling is an exchange of money that generates no real economic gain. It produces no commodity. No matter who is to gain, there must be an equal loss for someone else.

And then there are the state lotteries. The one principle upon which state lotteries are based is that the state must receive a great deal more money than it pays out. In other words, the state skims quite a large amount off the top.

"And that," Henry explained, "is what the Mafia also does. It takes money off the top from the numbers game in Harlem in the same way that it does from the roulette tables in Vegas. It is big business. Whenever anyone transgresses the code of the Mafia, the Mafia has agents to bring the transgressor to account for his actions. Those people are as thorough as the IRS.

"I presume the police are entertaining the possibility that Mrs. Gaulton angered the Mafia and has been put in cold storage by one of their agents."

"Who perhaps looked like a possum," Harriet murmured vaguely—a comment I did not understand.

"If you say so," Henry said, undeterred in his lecture. "There is no real difference between the state lotteries and what goes on in the casinos, except the uses to which the profits are put. The principles are the same as far as the working of the game itself goes. Both the Mafia and the state are out to take the suckers."

I sensed that probably Harriet was tired of Henry's harangue.

"Thank you for an excellent lecture, Henry," I said. "But this is Harriet's birthday. She doesn't want to hear you spin out your theories and opinions."

"Now, Helen, don't fuss at your good-looking husband," Harriet objected. "I'm just fascinated by everything he says."

The remark was characteristic of Harriet and the role to which she had been bred.

After the waitress had taken our empty dishes, Betty Kyrides came with the cake I had ordered—flaming, not with ninety candles, but perhaps with a third that many, forming the numerals nine and zero. Harriet's eyes were as bright as the candles when she caught sight of the cake.

As Betty began the Happy Birthday song, other diners joined in. Harriet acknowledged their well wishes with a gracious little wave of the hand.

She did not get all the candles blown out on the first try, or on the second; but at the third attempt, all wicks, though smoking, were out. The candles were removed, and at length Betty cut the cake.

Harriet insisted on sending a slice to each diner in the restaurant. For seven or eight minutes the entire restaurant became an impromptu party for Harriet. She radiated delight.

When we arrived again at her house, Henry handed her out of the Pontiac. After effusive thanks for our remembrance of her birthday, she permitted Henry to escort her to her door. I heard her say, "These men from the Mafia—what kind of car would one of them drive?"

"I don't know, Mrs. Bushrow," Henry replied. "Cadillac? Lincoln, or maybe a Kharman Ghia—something fancy?"

"You would expect that," she said.

She went into the house, and the door closed.

IX

What I Saw at the Grocery Counter!

VERA McKENDRY

I know it would not have bothered me if it had happened to any organization except the Music Club in any town except Borderville. But I was bothered a great deal by the way the Monica Gaulton scandal just kept coming up in the press. It got worse and worse, and I couldn't help thinking that a good many of our members blamed me somehow for the notoriety that had sullied our beautiful fashion show.

I was standing with my cart at the check-out counter at Kroger's one morning when I heard a woman several places ahead of me exclaim, "Look at that!" I saw a hand reach out and take one of those trashy scandal sheets from the rack.

After a moment's pause, the woman next in line said, "I'll have to have one too." And I saw her hand reach out and take another copy of the same wretched thing.

I suppose I should count myself lucky that there was one copy of *The American Exposé* left on the rack by the time I got to it. There on the front of that disgraceful thing was a picture of a much younger Monica Gaulton in a very abbreviated outfit with a headline reading, "Was NY Chanteuse Killed by Wealthy Southern Family?"

I was horrified. For weeks Borderville had speculated about the effect of Monica Gaulton's death upon the Gaulton estate. No one could imagine that the Gaulton children regretted Monica's removal from the list of probable heirs. But we had no thought of laying the guilt of murder at the doorstep of any of the family. At least I hoped we hadn't.

There it was—in bold red letters: "Was NY Chanteuse Killed by Wealthy Southern Family?"

But to appreciate my feelings in this matter fully, you will have to read the story itself.

AMERICAN EXPOSÉ

Was NY Chanteuse Killed by
Wealthy Southern Family?
  That was on the front cover. Inside it said:

MUSIC CLUB MURDER

Did Family Kill Monica Tay?
Borderville, Tenn., Nov. 12.

  Police are investigating the possibility that members of the socially prominent Gaulton family may have poisoned the glamorous Monica Tay, faded star of New York stage and cabaret, to prevent her inheriting the Gaulton fortune.

  Tay, wife of the wealthy furniture manufacturer, Douglass Gaulton, was found dead in Borderville's fashionable First Presbyterian Church a short time ago. The coroner reported cyanide.

Family Resented Outsider
  "There was a lot of money in it," said a long-time friend of the murdered woman. After an extended absence Tay had returned to her hometown to marry its leading industrialist. "When you think of all that money, you can see

why the family might want her out of the way," our informant observed. "I don't say they did it, but some think so."

Fortune in the Millions

The assets of Gaultwood, a leading industry in this Appalachian community, are estimated conservatively at tens of millions of dollars.

Old Scandal Revived?

It is rumored here that thirty years ago Tay gave birth to the illegitimate child of a prominent business figure. Did the father at last marry Tay in 1990? Octogenarian Douglass Gaulton, totally paralyzed and speechless as the result of a massive stroke in 1991, is unlikely to tell us.

Where There's a Will

Rumor has it that a will drawn by Gaulton after the marriage would have left the entire estate to the murdered woman. It is speculated that members of Gaulton's family were privy to the will. Suspicion is now cast upon family members who would have been in line for megabucks.

There it was—another example of Appalachian decadence! The way we are treated by the national press is infuriating. This specimen was merely the extreme. There was no mention of the fact that our fashion show was put on to support music scholarships. There was no mention that we have an excellent college—and a ballet company—and that our wonderful Loft Theater is in Ambrose Courthouse just eighteen miles from Borderville.

And to think! That horrible *Exposé* was on the rack at

every checkout counter in every grocery store from Maine to Hawaii.

I would have been devastated to think that all this sensation could develop at any time. But that it should happen while I was president of the club? Oh, no!

X

The Moonlighters

HARRIET GARDNER BUSHROW

Every time I asked myself who could have wanted to murder Monica, I just had to say: almost anybody. That was the kind of woman she was.

I think it would have been easier to get hold of what happened if I hadn't known anything at all about Monica. But I had known her. I admit that she was only a girl then, and that people change—but I couldn't see that she had changed for the better. And so, because I knew her, I could believe that almost anybody might want to kill Monica Gaulton.

That left me looking, not for people to add to the list of folks that might want to get rid of her, but for some way to make the list shorter.

Well then, who could have got into the house to put the cyanide in Doug's whiskey flask? Here is the list:

Three nurses
Any of the Gaultons
The man who looked like a possum and had a car with
    one brown fender
Those people who danced around in the moonlight in
    Gaulton's backyard

Take the three nurses—the one I knew best was little Mrs. Greene, but I had seen the others. There was Miss Thorpe—tall, skinny woman—pale blue eyes, pale complexion, pale everything. If you said boo to her, she would fade away. She comes in at four and stays on duty until midnight.

I don't know much about the other nurse—Mrs. Thompson. She comes on duty when Miss Thorpe goes off, and stays until Mrs. Greene gets to the house at eight in the morning.

I have to admit that any one of those women had the run of the place and could have got to that flask with nobody the wiser.

But there it was. I knew two of the women, and I just couldn't believe that either of them would kill anyone—not even Monica.

Well, what about the Gaultons? Family, you see—they would come and go as they please—nothing unusual about that. It would be so normal for any of them to go in and out of that house that no one would take any notice. But, again, I knew the family, and I just didn't want to think that one of them would do such a horrible thing. Poison! A Gaulton would never think of a thing like that. One of them might have shot Monica or hit her in the head with a doorstop. But poison is so sly and sneaky!

Yet all of these people on my list might have as much knowledge about the flask as the Gaultons did, and certainly the Gaultons had reason to despise Monica—but . . . !

That *but* again! *But* I knew them. *But* I had formed an idea about their character. *But* I just couldn't see any of them as the killer of Monica Taybrook Gaulton.

So I have to admit that it would have been easier to get at the mystery if I hadn't known a thing about any of the suspects at the start.

Now, what about the ones I did not know? There was the possum-like man with one brown fender. I think I wanted him to be the murderer—and that is almost as bad as saying the Gaultons couldn't have done it because I know them.

Still he was the only person Olive actually had seen go into Doug's house the morning of the day Monica died. That meant that this man with the brown fender was somebody we really needed to know something about.

And Olive had said—why did I set so much store by what Olive said? She is really a silly old goose—does needlework, watches TV, and looks out the window. Well, what else can the poor dear do?

Did she *really* see those people standing in a ring in the moonlight in Doug's backyard or did she see it on TV?

I had decided that she had actually seen them because the one connection she has with real life is keeping up with that neighborhood through the window. And besides, she talked about it with her rector.

Now that was a situation where you might say prior opinion was helpful—because, you see, Olive has passed on loads of gossip to me over the years, and I have rarely known her to be wrong as to facts, though sometimes she drew surprising conclusions from them. As for Monica—nothing she might have been up to would have surprised me.

So was it witchcraft? Are we ready for that in Borderville? I am sure all of us have read about cults and strange things like devil worship, and ritual sacrifice of animals, and I don't know what-all. Was Monica mixed up in that kind of thing? I wouldn't put it past her, but it needed looking into.

So I went over to Doug's house to talk to Mrs. Greene.

Oh yes, she said, it was all true. Miss Thorpe had told her about it. Twelve young people (six couples) and Monica. That made thirteen, and Mrs. Greene seemed to think that was important.

77

"What were they doing?" I asked. There had to be some plan of business—like a club, perhaps?

She said they sometimes sat around on the floor in the living room. Miss Thorpe had reported that they used a blue light and made moaning noises as they swayed one way and another. Miss Thorpe said that whenever there was one of these meetings, she could feel a cold presence.

"And the whole thing is connected some way with crystals," Mrs. Greene said. "The crystals are in her room right now."

"Crystals?" I knew about looking into a crystal ball, but this must be something different. "What kind of crystal?"

"I'll show them to you."

Mrs. Greene led me through the bathroom to the next bedroom. Monica's room was the one that used to be Virginia's; the furniture had been modern in the thirties. There was a very nice walnut bed—veneer, no doubt—a highboy—also walnut—and a dresser: a suite. On the dresser there was a tortoiseshell set of hand mirror, comb, and brush like we used to have. I am sure it was Iris's, because you would never find a set like that nowadays.

There was a little slipper chair and a recliner, which was new and didn't go with anything else in the room. There was also a writing table with a matching chair.

On this writing table there was—I don't know what you would call it. It was a kind of specimen, I guess. Anyway, it was crystals, all clustered together looking as if they were coming out of the rock that was the base of it.

"What do they do with the crystals?"

Mrs. Greene shook her head in wonderment. "I truly cannot say," she declared. She knew only what Miss Thorpe told her. She thought it had something to do with the phases of the moon, because they went out into the backyard and did strange things when it was clear on a moonlit night.

I admit that there was something fascinating about that chunk of rock with all those crystals just bursting out of it and all those surfaces with light reflecting differently from each one of them.

"I've got to know more about this," I said. "This must be that business that I hear about on TV—there must be some way to find out. I don't suppose Mrs. Gaulton had some books about it?"

Mrs. Greene didn't know.

"Perhaps if I looked in the drawer of her writing table—" I said, and before Mrs. Greene could say Jack Robinson, I pulled open the drawer. It wasn't a thing a lady would do, but I did it.

For once I was lucky. In the drawer was Monica's memorandum book and next to it some little volumes: *Matriarchal Priesthood* by Delois Charleroi, *Crystals and the Life Force* by Quanta Elaka, and *Chanelling for Self and Others* by Lura Erni.

Aha! Just what I was looking for. "I'm going to borrow these," I said. They were small enough that I could jam them into my purse.

There was something else in that drawer. It had a couple of tiny batteries and a jumble of wire. I had no idea what it might be and pushed it aside. Then way at the back, rolled up, there was a kind of certificate or diploma printed on paper that looked like parchment. When I got this thing unrolled, I saw that it had six-pointed stars, crescents, and crosses all over it—and some marks I couldn't recognize. At the top, it said, LIFE FORCE INSTITUTE OF CALIFORNIA. And below that it certified that Monica Gaulton was a channel of the third order. Now I leave it to you to tell me just what that means.

The parchment rerolled itself, and I placed it in the drawer again. I turned around, ready to leave, because I could hardly wait to see what was in those little books.

79

Mrs. Greene said, "Do you want to see the robe Mrs. Gaulton wore when those young people were here?"

The door to Monica's closet was open—just the way it was, no doubt, when she left the house to go to the Music Club Fashion Show. On a wire hanger there was something extraordinary.

It was a gown or robe of a blue, silky material—but rather stiff. It was slightly full and hung straight down from a gold lamé yoke that was the most gorgeous thing you ever saw.

That garment looked like something Hindu or Egyptian and had sequins sewed right thick at the bottom, and they played out gradually up to about the waist. If Monica made that thing herself, she must have inherited more patience from her mother than I would have expected. I tell you I wouldn't want to put all that handwork on anything.

I handed the robe back to Mrs. Greene, said good-bye, went downstairs, and came back to the real world. Poor Doug! To think that someone like Monica Taybrook had snared him.

As soon as I got home, I went right to work on the books. And the things I learned!

First there was the little memorandum book, a notebook with a brown cover, the kind that you open from the bottom like a calendar. On the first page she had written her name—Monica Tay—and her address in Las Vegas. That was done with a blue ballpoint. Then, in the same blue ballpoint, there were some addresses. I'll write it all down just the way she had it in the little notebook.

Monica Tay
Room 38
The Desert Winds Motel
Las Vegas, Nevada

                    Pistol Pete's   321-6184
                    Water Hole   321-5923
                    Dry Gulch   321-4027
                    Al   321-9214
                    Tina   321-0635
                    212-877-6943

All of that was written by the same blue ballpoint. Everything after that was in black or in pencil. Here is the rest of it.

                    Edna   968-2563
                    968-7216
                    968-7412

                    Mark   395-2786
                    Sean   479-4316
                    Greg   479-6328
                    Larry   395-5069
                    Wayne   479-5324
                    Tim   395-9217
                    212-563-9174

I am going to say something about these numbers later on. Maybe you would want to turn the page down so you can refer to the numbers in a hurry.

There was a lot to learn from that little notebook, but it would take a good deal of time to work it all out, and I was too excited to do it just then. I wanted to get into the books about this New Age, and I couldn't wait!

The books were very "educational."

Did you know that quartz crystals store a power that runs in lines from one point to the other? And did you know that you can generate power for your crystals by setting them out in the sun—or in the moonlight—or in salt water?

I didn't know any of that.

I have these cut crystal beads that Lamar gave me when we were married, and I never thought about setting them out in the sunlight or putting them in salt water, though there have been times when I wore them in the moonlight with good effect.

But my beads aren't "terminate," which seems to mean "pointed." So I don't suppose there is any way the Life Force can get into them or run out of them, unless possibly the fact that there's a string that goes through them might help.

Well I just never knew all that about crystals, although I do remember when Lamar had a crystal radio set and some kind of energy certainly ran through that thing.

Oh, I just learned so much! Sunlight is masculine, and moonlight is feminine. I don't know what that does to the man in the moon, but I do know that we women have been using moonlight to our advantage ever since Eve.

Somehow by using these crystals, a person can channel all that force into herself or into somebody else. And that gets your inner consciousness going and opens up your "potential." Then your "true self" will come out.

And here I have spent most of my life modestly trying to hide my true self! I just didn't know how dreadful that was.

There is something called Kundalini energy and "endless knowledge."

And guess what? Delois Charleroi says that the power to do all this is partial to women. So women are the natural priestesses of the Life Force. She goes into all sorts of ideas that once would have been embarrassing, but now you see all about yeast infections on television every day; and I guess, as we sang back in the twenties, "Lordy knows: anything goes!"

I couldn't read that stuff all in one day. It was more than my weak brain could take in at one time. After a while it had made me so sleepy that I had to go to bed, but the next day I went at it again until I had a pretty good idea what Monica had been up to. And I can tell you that I am just as happy that my parents brought me up to be a Presbyterian.

All of that rigmarole was very interesting as applied to the mystery; and while I didn't find anything that would explain why somebody put cyanide in Monica's whiskey, I could see that she had been mixed up with some mighty peculiar doings. And all that tommyrot showed me a way to operate, as I shall now explain.

After I had soaked up as much of that nonsense as I could without going nutty, I looked back at the memorandum book.

The thing that struck me there was the group of six names at the end—just the given names, and all of them male. Now don't jump to any conclusions. I didn't think for a minute that Monica was into a sex racket. Something of that kind could never be kept a secret very long in Borderville. With six men on the list, it struck me that maybe there was a wife for each man, and that would make twelve people in all, don't you see.

Now twelve is the number mentioned on page 27 of Delois Charleroi's book, *Matriarchal Priesthood.*

Twelve people and Monica would make thirteen. And if you get thirteen people dancing in a ring in the moonlight and Olive sees them—well, it's little wonder the poor dear thought about demons and witchcraft.

That kind of thing just isn't supposed to happen in Borderville. The town is simply overrun with Baptists, Methodists, Presbyterians, and a few Episcopalians, not to mention the Church of Christ and the Disciples. Why we've even got a Catholic church here. Holy Rollers are as far out as we ever get.

But Monica had been up north, and, worse than that, she had been out in Vegas and who knows where else.

There they were. Six young couples, no doubt—just the age when they ought to be putting their roots down deep into real church life, getting good strong values, starting their little families instead of hobnobbing with the likes of Monica Taybrook Gaulton.

It was a pity she had not written out their full names. But that didn't really matter. I had their numbers. What did they call it in the Bible? The number of the beast, if I recall.

XI

MURDERED WOMAN NEVER A MOM

Police Department Gives Lie to Gossip Rag

Police Chief Steve Roper advised the *Banner-Democrat* yesterday that the report of the autopsy conducted on the body of the late Mrs. Monica Gaulton revealed that the murdered woman had never borne a child. This information was released as a result of an unsupported innuendo made in the most recent issue of *The American Exposé*.

"The suggestion in *The American Exposé* is absolutely false," Roper said. "The police have never received allegations that Douglass Gaulton might have fathered a child upon Monica Taybrook in the 1960s or at any other time."

Asked how the rumor may have reached the tabloid, which is based in Chicago, the Borderville officer replied, "Damned if I know."

A *Banner-Democrat* reporter interviewed William Douglass Gaulton, Jr., an executive of Gaultwood, regarding questions raised in the *Exposé* article. "I hesitate to dignify such slander with a denial; but no, my grandfather did not have an extramarital affair with Monica Taybrook at any time."

The young Monica Taybrook worked briefly in the office of Gaultwood in 1952 before going to New York to pursue a career on the stage. Four years ago she returned to Borderville and married her former employer. As Mrs. Douglass Gaulton she made many friends among the social elite of this city. Her death by poison on October 27 remains a mystery.

Asked whether his family was considering suit against the Chicago publication, young Gaulton replied: "We did consider it. Our position now is that the charge is so outrageous as to be ridiculous."

Douglass Gaulton, about whom the innuendos were made, is eighty-seven years old and has been incapacitated by a massive stroke for the last fourteen months. "No, we did not tell my grandfather about the insinuations in *The American Exposé*," the grandson replied to the *Banner-Democrat*'s question.

Chief Roper reports that his department is actively pursuing the investigation of Mrs. Gaulton's murder.

XII

A Transaction at Ambrose Courthouse

HENRY DELAPORTE

On November 15, Mr. James Neville came to my office and asked me to represent his son Geoff, who was in some trouble about an automobile.

Jim Neville is a Rotarian whom I have known for more than twenty years. He has the largest appliance business in this area, with branch stores in Cooksport and Ambrose Courthouse.

When his boy Geoff, whom I remember as a Little Leaguer, graduated from college a few years ago, Jim put him in charge of the Ambrose Courthouse branch.

Ambrose Courthouse is an attractive historic Virginia town a matter of eighteen miles from Borderville. The reader may know it as the home of the famous Loft Theater, a professional playhouse founded during the Great Depression that has since acquired a national reputation.

But Ambrose Courthouse is a limited market for appliances; and Jim thought it might be a good place for young Geoff, fresh out of Randolph Macon with an arts degree, to learn the business.

Having had no previous experience, Geoff has made a number of mistakes. The gravest of these had to do with the purchase of a car, the results of which had just burst into full bloom.

What happened was that some four years ago a woman came into the store to look at dishwashers. She priced them extensively and took notes.

A person of a certain maturity, she was both plausible and personable. The conversation she struck up with Geoff became confidential as well as extended.

The woman said that she had been living in Las Vegas, where she had run a secretarial bureau, but that she was moving back to Virginia to stay with her aging mother, whose health was declining.

There was a story about the financial sacrifice she was making, but of course family obligations came first. She had sold all the furniture she had had in her Vegas apartment, because, of course, her mother's house was furnished with everything—except a dishwasher—and now she was puzzled about what to do with her car because her mother had a late-model Chrysler.

Her own car, which she had driven from Las Vegas, was a nice little Dodge Dart with only 16,000 miles on it. She liked it very much.

But there was really no need for her to keep it, and she thought she might let it go.

It would be just the thing as a second car for a young couple.

At that point an idea popped into the head of Geoff Neville. It so happened that he and his wife had been married only a matter of nine months, and his wife, being now three months pregnant, would certainly be needing transportation of her own after the baby came.

Devoted to his bride and proud of his own forthcoming fatherhood, he saw the opportunity to obtain for his wife a Dodge Dart, possibly at a much reduced price. And on the other hand, this lady from Las Vegas would obviously be glad to sell.

Where was the car? It was just outside the shop.

Geoff looked the car over. It seemed to be everything the woman had said it was.

She named her own price.

Geoff calculated briefly. He realized that he had stumbled upon a remarkable bargain.

The woman produced the papers, which appeared to be in order. She accompanied Geoff to the Ambrose County Trust Bank, where he secured a loan. From there the two crossed the street to the courthouse, from which the city gets its name, and the transfer of title was made.

Now, four years later, Geoff had attempted to trade in the Dodge Dart on a station wagon. It was the engine number that gave it all away.

What Geoff had was a motor vehicle stolen from the Rentz Car people. This particular vehicle had been rented to a certain Monique Towson and had not been heard from since. The papers that Miss or Mrs. Towson had shown to Geoff and had been accepted at the courthouse were apparently forged.

Geoff was in possession of a stolen car. Without much trouble we were able to show that the boy had bought the Dart in good faith and that he was not liable for any little dents the young Mrs. Neville may have incurred as she drove her two children (oh, yes, she had a second child now) hither and thither about Ambrose Courthouse. Nor could he be held responsible for the mileage that had thus accrued.

My immediate suspicion was that Monique Towson was none other than Monica Taybrook Gaulton. As soon as I had Geoff's whole story, I arranged to show him the picture of Mrs. Gaulton from the account of her death in the *Banner-Democrat*; and in the process of securing the clipping from my wife, I was reminded by her—as though I might have forgotten—that Monica Taybrook came in her most recent peregrination to Tennessee from Las Vegas. Moreover, my wife declared that in the light of things she had heard in a recent conversation with Mrs. Lamar Bushrow, the theft of a car was thoroughly in character with what was known of the late Monica Gaulton.

The clipping with the picture of Mrs. Gaulton was readily found; and although the newspaper cut was none too clear, as soon as I showed it to Geoff, he said, "That's her."

I, of course, passed this information on to the police lieutenant in charge of the investigation. In a matter of a week, he had the courtesy to report that Mrs. Gaulton had indeed been traced to Las Vegas, that she had in effect stolen the Rentz car, and moreover that she had lost heavily at the casinos, as had been generally rumored.

Information about the theft somehow got to the *Banner-Democrat* and caused an additional flurry of interest.

My wife and Mrs. Bushrow are satisfied that the theft has been fully explained. And Mrs. Bushrow, at least, says that she is not surprised.

This particular episode does not contribute to the explanation of the mystery of Mrs. Gaulton's death. But the aforementioned ladies insist that it adds to the picture and that there is a tie-in with certain information which came to light somewhat later.

I did not wish to clutter this account by inserting the above episode, but I was positively commanded to do so and have consequently complied.

In fact, the price which Mrs. Gaulton quoted to Geoff Neville was so low that Geoff should certainly have suspected that there was something wrong with the deal. Charity demands, however, that we attribute his purchase of stolen property to innocence rather than guile. He is young and needed the car. He asked no further questions. He is no doubt wiser now. In the final analysis, he took a loss that equaled the trade-in value of the car. But against his loss we must consider his four years' use of the vehicle.

Beyond doubt, the Rentz people had insurance; and all loss was ultimately absorbed in the premiums that the rest of us pay.

If there is a lesson here, it is that the whole community is damaged when one member breaks the law.

We hear much of victimless crime. I doubt that there is such an offense.

XIII

THEFT OF RENTAL CAR BY GAULTON

It was revealed yesterday that Monica Tay-brook Gaulton, murdered here last month, stole a rental automobile shortly before she appeared in Borderville four years ago.

The glamorous image of Monica Gaulton, whose mysterious death by cyanide poisoning shook Borderville society, unraveled somewhat Thursday when a Dodge Dart, rented under an assumed name from the Rentz Rental Car agency of Las Vegas, Nevada, was found in Ambrose Courthouse. Evidence indicated that Monica Taybrook, subsequently married to Douglass Gaulton, had sold the vehicle to Geoffrey Neville, son of James Neville, of Borderville, Va.

Purchaser of Stolen Car Shocked

"It was really a shock to me," said Geoffrey Neville when interviewed by the *Banner-Demo-crat*. "She seemed such a nice lady." Neville, 25, is the manager of Neville's Appliances of Am-brose Courthouse, owned by the senior Neville.

The car in question, a 1988 Dodge Dart, was rented by a Monique Towson from the Rentz agency in Las Vegas, Nevada, and never returned. The theft became apparent when Neville attempted to sell the car to Elwood Duncan of Ambrose County.

Friends of Society Figure Incredulous

"I simply don't believe it," said Mrs. Michael F. Brandon, board member of the Borderville Country Club. "Monica was such an open person. It is impossible to think of her in this light."

Mrs. Horace McKendry, president of the Borderville Music Club, whose annual fashion show Gaulton was preparing to M.C. when she succumbed, was reluctant to talk to our reporter. "All I can say is that we had no idea of anything of this sort," she stated.

Gaulton, under the name of Monica Tay, is said to have enjoyed an extensive career on and off Broadway. She was married three years ago to Douglass Gaulton, financier and business leader of this city.

Returned to Borderville "Penniless"

According to Edna Finch, proprietor of the Cup and Saucer Café and long-time friend of the murdered woman, Mrs. Gaulton returned to Borderville four years ago penniless. "She lost a lot of money out there," Finch stated. "All she had was one dollar and fifteen cents and an Exxon card in her purse and that Dodge." Finch speculated that Taybrook, later to be Gaulton, had used the money from the sale of the automobile for living expenses.

XIV

The December Meeting of
the Borderville Music Club

HARRIET GARDNER BUSHROW

I am not a member of the Borderville Music Club. Whatever talent I may have runs in some other direction. Vera
McKendry, the club president, gave me a special invitation
to attend the December meeting. She didn't say why; but
there was to be a program of organ music by Helen Delaporte, and when I heard that, you couldn't have kept me
away with a ten-foot fence.

Of course I know quite a number of the women in the
club—the older ones, naturally. Some are in the DAR with
me, and some are Rotary Anns, and some are Presbyterians. Then I used to be active in the YWCA and the
Women's Council and all those other things. One of the
nice things about living in a town like Borderville is that I
can be right at home in any group.

The meeting was in the parish hall at the Episcopal
church. They had a lovely social hour with every kind of
refreshment before they started the meeting. Vera warned
me that I had better not eat much before I came because
that social hour would just about take the place of breakfast
and lunch as well. And she was right.

The table was set up along one side of the parish hall. I
believe it was Mrs. Rosenberry, Mrs. DeMoss, Edwina
Houseman, and Margaret Cornette who were the hostesses;

and I must say they had outdone themselves. There was a beautiful lace cloth on the table, and Edwina has this lovely silver epergne that supports four or five glass bowls, each bowl filled with little bunches of holly. And of course, there were red candles—all very pretty.

Somebody had found the sweetest little paper napkins with gold harps and bells and of course holly leaves.

And the food was *so* good!

There was coffee and hot chocolate and little finger sandwiches with some kind of salmon paste in them, and a dip with raw cauliflower, which isn't too good for my teeth. And then there was the best salad. It is the Asheville salad, if you know what that is. And then there were lovely cakes. Helen was absolutely right about those refreshments.

So after we had nibbled all we could, we went over to where some folding chairs had been set up for the meeting.

Mrs. McKendry rapped with her little gavel while all the ladies fished around in their handbags for their yearbooks, so they could have the club collect, which was all about music and how fine it is. I remember one thing they said: it was about music and harmony—about being "rightly tuned instruments" in the way we live. And a little bit later in the meeting we needed something like that.

One of the ladies went to the piano to play so the club could sing the Federation Hymn. I was not familiar with it. There are a few gentlemen with good strong voices in the club. And with all those musicians singing together it was just a choir.

The recording secretary read the minutes of the November meeting. Lo and behold, the club had voted to purchase a gift for me and one for Helen because of what we did for the fashion show!

They needn't have got anything for me; for I have to admit that I had the best time of anyone at the show. And that's what I told them when they gave me this beautiful box with a lovely big bow on it. Inside was a quaint little Toby jug—Royal Doulton! So you can see it was expensive.

Then the corresponding secretary read a letter from a member who had regretfully resigned and the club voted to accept the resignation.

The treasurer gave her report of the final figures from that famous fashion show, and they all seemed pleased that they had made so much money.

Then there was some old business. After that was over, Mrs. McKendry called for new business.

Who should get up but Tolah Stalker! She is one person who can't be avoided—no matter how hard you try.

I suppose there is one in every town. I don't know why it is, but she has to be in everything. If there is an office that nobody will accept, Tolah is right there and willing to take it; so she gets the job. And that's how she got to be past president of this and past secretary of that and so on.

I suppose she must have been an officer in the Music Club sometime in the past because she was acting like it belonged to her.

"Now is as good a time to talk about this thing as any," she said.

It seems to me there was an old woman who threw an apple at somebody back in Roman times or something like that—apple of discord, I think they called it. Well if that is what the apple was, Tolah was the one that threw it.

"I don't like to see the name of my club in a rag like *The American Exposé*. I don't like to go into my grocery store when there at the checkout counter I see 'Music Club Murder.' I want to know who is responsible for the bad publicity we've been getting. How did that scandal sheet get its information?" My, how she did go on!

Nobody said anything for a minute. That is the way it always is when Tolah starts one of her tirades.

Then Mrs. McKendry said—you could tell she was annoyed—"I don't know that anyone was responsible."

"Well, it is intolerable!" Tolah tossed her head.

Little Mrs. Grayson spoke up, trying to smooth things over a bit. "I'm sure it is very unpleasant. I don't know why the grocery store sells those papers." Several ladies joined in and said, "Isn't it awful!" and that kind of thing.

And then—

"Who asked that Gaulton woman to have anything to do with our fashion show in the first place?" Only Tolah could have said a thing like that.

Well, the room was just very quiet.

Then Ernestine Fuller replied in her soft little voice, "If you want to know, Tolah, I was chairman of that committee, and I asked her."

Then Tolah said, "I seem to remember that it was you who brought her into the club in the first place. I just think you had better make inquiries next time before you get someone of her character to represent the club."

That's our Tolah!

"I am saying this for the good of the club," she added.

At this point private conversations broke out all over the room. Everybody had something to whisper to her neighbor—most of it, I would imagine, about Tolah.

Madam Chairman then very wisely announced that we would all adjourn to the sanctuary for the program. So we all trooped off to hear Helen play the organ.

I am no expert on church architecture, but I would say that Presbyterians go in for a lot more light than Episcopalians do. But it was bright enough in there for me to get a good look at those kneelers like the one Olive has been working on. The several that had been installed were exquisite, but nothing as fancy as Olive's.

Well, I must say Helen has a wonderful touch on that

organ. And when the concert was over, so many ladies were congratulating the performer that I thought: *I'll give Helen a call from home later and have a nice little chat with her then.* So that's what I did.

"Helen," I said, "your numbers were simply lovely."

She laughed and said, "Thank you, Harriet. Did you like the Widor?"

Now what is a Widor? Helen knows I haven't the first idea about music. So I said it was lovely and changed the subject.

"Of course Tolah Stalker is one of nature's mistakes," I said, "but the fact remains that those *Exposé* people got their story from somebody. Do you suppose they got it from the woman at the Cup and Saucer?"

Helen knew all about that because Henry Delaporte had been hired by Bill Gaulton to see whether they could bring suit for slander.

Helen said that Edna Finch swore she had not talked to anybody from the *Exposé,* though she must surely have been the source. The Gaultons, however, decided not to do anything about it, because Henry Delaporte said that apart from the expense, a suit against an outfit like the *Exposé* can go on so long that Doug Gaulton would be dead before it ever came to court.

And then she told me about how Monica had swindled Norman and Conrad out of all that money, claiming each of them was responsible for her being in trouble, when she wasn't pregnant at all. Helen got that, you see, from Henry; and she made me promise not to tell anyone. But since Janet herself revealed it all in Chapter VI, I guess I'm not talking out of school when I mention it.

Henry had told Helen the police had found Doug's will right away—leaving everything to Monica, of course. And because of the will, they kept coming back to the Gaultons and questioning them over and over.

After we had finished our little conversation, I got to thinking about Monica's life. That girl turned out to be a swindler and blackmailer and a seducer and a thief. It was all so sad. Of course, she probably went to the reward she deserved. But somebody had killed her, and we would never hear the end of it until we knew who that person was.

XV

A Conversation with Ernestine Fuller

HELEN DELAPORTE

I don't know why I ever agreed to play a program for the
Music Club in the month of December. An organist for an
Episcopalian congregation has more than she can do at two
times of the year: Easter and Christmas. On Christmas Eve
there is always an hour's concert followed by the midnight
service. Then there is the service on Christmas itself, and
twelve days later there is Epiphany, not to mention the Sun-
days between. If Christmas should fall on a Thursday, the
result for the organist is at least five services in fourteen
days.

On the other hand, the Music Club didn't seem to mind
that I used for their program compositions I had recently
played for a Sunday church service; and I could of course
perform for the Music Club a few of the things I was preparing for midnight mass on the twenty-fourth.

I am always so busy in December that I don't have time
for other problems. I was, however, quite distressed over
what Tolah Stalker said at the club meeting.

I was not there when the unpleasantness flared up, because I had gone into the sacristy to change into my organ
shoes and get ready to begin my program as soon as the
business meeting was over. Afterwards I hadn't been at

home more than ten minutes before my phone began to ring.

It was a succession of calls, not about my playing, but about Tolah. The reaction of the members varied from dismay to indignation. I got all sorts of reports of Tolah's comments, but at the mildest possibility they must have been outrageous.

After I had been on the line for about two hours, I had a call from Daphne Riggs.

"Helen, you've got to do something," she began—no greeting—no identifying herself. "Ernestine is going to resign from the club."

Busy as I was, why was I the one who had to do something about it? On the other hand, if Daphne thought I was the one who *could* do something about it, it was obvious that I had been nominated.

So I called Ernestine.

She was very subdued when she answered the phone.

I explained that I had not been in the room when Tolah ignited the fireworks, but that I had heard about it from five very concerned people.

This information, of course, had little good effect on Ernestine's spirits. She insisted that it would be best for the club if she resigned.

"Why?" I demanded. "You couldn't have known what would happen."

"It's not that," she said. "I made such a mess of the fashion show from the very beginning."

"But you didn't!" I insisted.

"Oh, I'm afraid I did."

"I don't know what you are talking about."

"I knew that Vera didn't like it when I told her I had asked Monica to be the M.C. But I went on anyway. I made a thing of Monica's big-time career in New York and all of that."

"I don't see anything there to be ashamed of. After all Monica *did* have a career, didn't she?"

There was a pause before Ernestine went on.

"Yes, you could say that; but it wasn't the career I told everyone it was, and it wasn't the career Monica told me it was."

Then the explanation came out.

Ernestine had a sorority sister who married a teacher at Brooklyn University. Like all the rest of us, the sorority sister inevitably saw a copy of *The American Exposé*. The mention of Borderville set off bells in the back of her mind, and the friend, out of curiosity, put through a call to Ernestine.

I suspect that it would have been a lesser shock to Ernestine if she had received the news in a letter. But in a conversation between old acquaintances much can come out that would never appear in writing.

Monica, so far as was known, had never appeared in any significant stage performance. But there was a bar around the corner from the building where the sorority sister and her husband had their apartment. And Monica had appeared there numerous times.

"And I told everybody that we had a star of Broadway as the M.C. of our fashion show," Ernestine wailed. "It makes me look so stupid."

So Monica Taybrook had gone to New York to become a success and had not made it. She had sung in second-rate bars as Monica Tay; and upon her return to us, through innuendo and outright untruth, Monica had made poor Ernestine believe that she was a luminary of considerable magnitude. Ernestine, in her enthusiasm, had innocently inflated the sham still further, and now she was as much ashamed of her own gullibility as she was hurt by Tolah's diatribe.

I did my best to tell her that we had all been taken in, but she said, No, Vera had obviously known from the beginning that Monica was a bad choice for anything the Music Club was sponsoring.

I finally persuaded Ernestine to wait at least a month before resigning from the club. In fact she did not resign, and only last March, Tolah herself withdrew from the club, to everyone's relief.

This episode added little to the ultimate solution of the mystery. But it is relevant to Monica's character. Consider it as if it were one of the pieces in a jigsaw puzzle, which, if omitted, would leave a gap in the picture.

XVI

Checking Up on the New Age

HARRIET GARDNER BUSHROW

That little memorandum book that I found in Monica's writing desk gave me a lot to think about. You may remember that a copy of it appeared on pages 80 and 81 of this book. Using a blue ballpoint pen, Monica had jotted down the phone numbers of six places. Three of them had names that showed that they couldn't be anything but bars in Las Vegas. And then there were two other Nevada numbers. But the sixth was a number in New York.

I have never been one to let my curiosity grow cool of its own accord. Those six numbers represented places where Monica was known—where people might tell me something about her. And I wanted to know lots of things.

Now I'm not rich. But one beautiful thing about being ninety years old is that you don't have to save for your old age anymore. Several years ago I added up the annuity Lamar left me, the little bit of money I have in the savings, the value of my house, and what I thought I might get for my furniture, which is no small item because all of my furniture is good stuff and over one hundred fifty years old. When I added to that my social security check, I realized I could probably take care of myself for the next eight or nine years and leave enough money to be buried decently. After that, I'll be in a place where I won't need to worry about money ever again.

So there was no reason why I couldn't spend a little something on phone calls to Nevada.

I rang up all the numbers in blue.

I didn't tell the people any lies—just said I was a friend of the family (true) and had found their number in Monica's memorandum book (true) and I was sorry to tell them that she was dead.

At all the places that I called, there were people who remembered Monica—though it took some time for the folks at the Dry Gulch to rustle up the one waiter who had been there when Monica was.

Everyone was sorry to hear she had passed on—what else could they say to a friend of the family? And I always asked if there was "anybody else I ought to call." There never was, which led me to believe that Monica hadn't talked very much about her personal life to people where she worked.

All told, I didn't learn a lot from anybody but Tina, and I got plenty from her.

She said she thought Monica showed up in Vegas about 1978. She never worked in any of the famous places, but put on her act in lounges and piano bars and so on. Then after a little while she went away and came back in 1986.

Tina said Monica had some money the first time she was in Vegas, but she played the tables a good bit and lost it all. It seemed she was bound and determined to get back everything she had lost, and get it back in the same way she had lost it—gambling—she was almost compulsive. She called it "revenge." So, whatever she made from her singing, she lost it all at the casinos. It was the same thing over and over again—get a little money, lose it all.

When Monica left Vegas for the last time, she cleared out without so much as a whisper to anybody. But Tina said she thought somebody that Monica was afraid of had shown up in Vegas.

"Do you have any idea who it was?" I asked.

"No idea," she said. It would be easy enough to get in bad with the rougher element in Vegas because there were plenty of that kind around. But she rather thought it was something about debt, because Monica was always borrowing or trying to borrow from someone and then having to hide. Tina thought maybe the money Monica lost when she first came to Vegas had something to do with it.

It was a good conversation I had with Tina.

The next number I called had a New York area code. If you'll look on page 81 again, you will notice that the last number listed there is also a New York number. The first of those numbers turned out to be her agency. Yes, they had represented Monica Tay, but they had not heard from her in three years; and that, of course, was how long she had been married to Doug Gaulton.

While I was at it, I thought I might as well ring the other New York number. The young woman who answered the phone informed me I had reached the Eldredge-Maningham Galleries. I knew immediately what that was, and pretended I was trying to locate and buy some Belter furniture. Yes, they had a "Belter group." I asked for a description, and without doubt it was Iris's living room furniture. I said I would get back to them.

All the other numbers in Monica's notebook were local numbers—in Virginia or Tennessee. One number was Edna's home; another was the Cup and Saucer Café. One was Dorothy's Beauty Shoppe, which later gave me a little bit of information.

And then there were the six young men.

As I said before, I saw right off what those names were. They represented her "New Age" pals. And I was right. They were all married, and that filled out Monica's New

Age circle to twelve people, and she, sure 'nuf, was the thirteenth.

When I tried the numbers, one line had been disconnected. Four of my calls were answered by those machines that nearly everyone has now. Ordinarily I hate those contraptions. They don't *answer;* they expect *you* to answer. And when I do answer, I feel like I'm talking to a brick wall. But those four answering machines told me quite a lot. I got the last names of all four couples. And with the given names that Monica had set down, I could get the addresses right out of the phone book. And aside from that, I got the names of the wives off two of the machines. I had caught quite a number of my fish without half trying.

And then, too, I had found out that most of those people were not from around here. You can laugh at me, but there are two kinds of people: those that are from here and those that are not. There was once a time when you could tell by the way someone talked that he was from New England, or Chicago, or some other place like that. But now, people move around so much—that is, people who work for the big corporations—that their children grow up not knowing exactly who they are or where they are from. They've heard so many different accents in so many different places that you can't always tell by their speech exactly where they were brought up. But I always know when folks are from Southwest Virginia or East Tennessee.

So what did I conclude? These were not yuppies. With their fresh young voices, they weren't old enough for that. No, they were children of yuppies. Monday through Friday, nine-to-five they were away from home—young husband and young wife working toward a lifestyle.

My lifestyle was given to me by my parents down in Georgia in the little community of Gloriosa—the church I went to, the school I attended, all those things. When I was a girl and went to a party, I could be sure it was the kind of party people approved of in Gloriosa. And my notions of behavior and misbehavior were the notions of Gloriosa.

For anyone who grows up in Borderville, Virginia-Tennessee, the community can still mean about the same that Gloriosa, Georgia, meant to me. But these yuppie youngsters move around so much that they have to get their lifestyle out of TV, which is the same everywhere; and it's really a pity.

Is it any wonder these rootless children fall prey to someone like Monica with that New Age trash!

Well, to get back on track—

There was this one child, who didn't have a job, because she was staying home. I thought: *Honey, you're the one for me.* But I was at a disadvantage, you see, because I didn't know her last name. All Monica had written down was "Wayne." So I asked Wayne's little wife if Dudley Spink was there.

She assured me that nobody of that name was living in that residence.

"Oh," I said (acting like I was at a loss, and I'm sure she could tell I was an old lady), "whose residence is this?"

Then she told me the full name, Wayne Archer.

I saw immediately that Mrs. Wayne Archer would be a likely source of information if I played my cards right. In the first place, she was at home during the day and I could probably get at her while she was alone. And in the second place, she had told me her name without the least hesitation, and I figured I could get her to tell me a great deal more. I would just wait a few days—time enough for her to forget about my call. Then I would pay her a visit and see what information she would give me.

Of course, I had to have an excuse for that visit.

Myrtis Johnson, who directs the Humane Society here, is in the DAR and several other organizations I belong to; and although the Humane people's campaign doesn't actually begin until March, I knew that Myrtis would help me if I explained. She was happy to oblige. She had lots of material and pledge cards and such items left over from last year. And she let me have that stuff and a little button that said "Humane Society" on it so that I would look very official. When I went to call on Mrs. Archer at 179 Ridgecroft Circle, I was set up for business.

It is a little bitty place—called, I believe, a town house. The apartment, hardly wide enough to park your car in front of it, had been there just long enough to need a little paint.

There was a front yard about as big as a pocket handkerchief and some little shrubs by the door, and there was nothing about the whole cluster of town houses to set them apart from town houses built in the same year anywhere else in the nation.

I thought: *Well, maybe dancing in a circle in the moonlight would be a relief from the push-button world of appliances, fast food, and the everlasting sound of that rock music—all of it with the same beat, the same instruments, the same loudness.* Two young people without much in their heads yet—cooped up on this monotonous street in their impersonal little apartment—someone like Monica could get her hands on them and they would not know what had happened to them.

The card just below the door bell read: TERRI AND WAYNE ARCHER. What a sweet name—Terri. I pressed the button and waited.

Terri is a pretty child—pregnant and looking like the baby would come any minute—the reason, I imagine, why she was not working. Has beautiful hair—auburn. It wasn't exactly combed; but then it is such a glorious color.

"I am collecting for the animal shelter," I said, "and I wondered if I could come in and talk to you for a minute."

I did not wait for an answer but just opened the screen door and walked in. Dear little Terri couldn't do a thing but stand back and let me step right in.

I sat myself down in the most comfortable chair in the little living room. I had all my material about the animal shelter ready, and poor Terri had as much chance of getting me out of that chair before I could pump her dry as a fish would have trying to whistle Dixie. I told her how many cats and dogs the shelter could accommodate—all that. Oh, I reeled it off at a great rate.

And all the time I was talking, my mind was on a paperback book on that child's coffee table. It caught my eye the minute I sat down. It was *Crystal Power and the Psyche*— black letters against a yellow cover—and the best I could see it, the author was that Quanta Elaka, the same one who wrote the book about crystals that I found in Monica's writing table.

I was just dying to say something about that; but I went on and on about the animal shelter and how it was a health measure as well as a convenience to keep strays off the street until finally Terri thought maybe she could pledge five dollars.

"Oh, darling, could you?"

Now, everybody knows that is just like giving fifty cents would have been forty years ago. And there I was acting like it was the donation of the year. What a hypocrite I am! But it was in a good cause.

So she went into the next room to get her checkbook. And while she was gone, I picked up *Crystal Power and the Psyche,* and it was just what I thought—written by that Quanta Elaka.

I was leafing through the book when Terri came back. She is really a sweet child. I hated to deceive her. But I went ahead anyway, and there really wasn't any harm in it.

"This is so interesting!" I said. "I suppose you know all about these different crystals."

"Well, yes—I know a little."

I said, "I have these crystal beads—cut crystal—it was very popular, and rather expensive, about the time I got married."

While I was talking, I was taking off my beads. I declare, when Lamar gave me that necklace, he never guessed what I would be doing with it all these years later.

"Look how the light shines on them. See, every color of the rainbow just dances in them!" And I moved the beads around a little to show them off.

Well, they really are crystal. I don't know how they are different from ordinary glass—something about the composition and the way they are cut. And the kind of crystal Quanta Elaka and those other people talk about is quartz. But that doesn't matter. This was just a way to get the girl to talk.

And sure enough it worked.

You never heard such a rapture about what a little old quartz rock can do. I said, "Yes," and "Un-huh," and "Isn't that remarkable." And between the two of us we had just a grand time.

"Well," I said, "now that you tell me all this, I venture to say that wearing these crystal beads might be the cause of me living such a long time; for you know, I am ninety years old."

Isn't it curious how I hated for people to know my age when I was forty, but now I am downright proud of being ninety? Well, the next thing I said was:

"Honey, would you let me borrow your book so I can read up on all this you are telling me? I'm afraid my old brain can't take all this in as fast as you are telling it."

"Oh, yes." She was pleased as Punch for me to take her

book. It was almost like a Jehovah's Witness when you agree to read their material.

"I'll take good care of it and bring it back soon."

"Oh, just keep it—you know—until you get through with it—okay?"

You never heard anybody as grateful as I was. And she needn't have worried about my bringing the book back—because that was the reason I borrowed it.

Well, I practically memorized the fool thing so that I could make all the right observations when I returned it to her, which I did a few days later. (I was afraid the stork might get there before I did, and that wouldn't be good at all because Terri would be so busy that she wouldn't have time for me or crystals or any other rubbish.)

"I have never read anything so amazing in my life," I said. And that was the truth. "This Quanta Elaka—such an unusual name. Is she Oriental?"

"Oh yes!" I could tell from the child's tone that being Oriental was better than being like the rest of us.

"She is Indian," the girl said. "Real Indian—not like 'Native American.'"

"How interesting! I think those people have such wisdom, don't you?"

"Yes," Terri agreed brightly. "We had a channel—our circle, that is—she has migrated." The poor child was trying to let me know that Monica wasn't with them anymore. "She—she was just full of all that wonderful—well, okay—you know, that LORE!" she said.

She went on and on about the channel of the third power! Yes indeed! It was Monica Gaulton, and she had migrated to another astral level, and that really wasn't a thing to be sorry or upset about, okay? Because that was what it was all about, okay?

The child rambled on like that for a couple of minutes, and I could see that Monica had really "done a number"—I believe that is what they they were calling it a few years back—had "done a number" on that circle that Olive saw dancing about in the moonlight.

Terri told me about going to Doug's house—"like just real old, and that big living room!"

The truth is that Doug's living room is almost as big as Terri's whole house, and I am sure that any building put up in 1927 is very old indeed to a child like Terri.

In a way I can understand the whole thing—the crystals, the channeling, the circle. In spite of all the wonders of modern education and all that TV has to offer, that child's generation never read enough fairy stories to get it out of their systems. So now that they are older, they yearn for the wonder.

She went on to tell me how the sun is the masculine principle and the moon is the feminine, and that was why the priestess had to be matriarchal—because the light from the sun is so strong that we can't actually look at it unless it is dimmed by clouds or the atmosphere, which takes all the good out of it somehow. But it seems that when the light is reflected from the moon, then it is ready for human digestion.

So the priesthood had to be matriarchal, and that meant that Monica had to be there to tell those poor kids what to do and when to do it. And if the priestess touched you, Terri assured me, you could just feel it tingling through your whole body (which made me think of that little battery and those wires I had seen in Monica's writing desk). And all the time, those kids thought they were exercising freedom of the will!

Then there was the other thing: gold is the sun, and silver is the moon. And just guess what! The channel of the third order needed to be recharged, not just by moonlight, but by money—Monica was actually milking those poor youngsters to the tune of a hundred dollars a month from each one of them—and the stars or the crystals or something else in the universe demanded silver or, even better, gold.

You know, lots of these young people wear gold chains. Both sexes now wear gold earrings. And of course there are gold watches and gold watchbands and all kinds of other gold jewelry. Monica had duped those children into bringing their precious metals to her so that she could absorb the power and transfer it to them.

Of course the gold and silver in those things that were brought to Monica were all turned into power to fill up her "channel," and those kids never saw any of it again.

I asked Terri what her circle was going to do now that their channel of the third power was no more.

Oh, she said, the circle had just come all to pieces before Monica "migrated." Some crazy woman had got hold of Mark Satterwhite and convinced him that the New Age was nothing but Satanism and that Monica was a Devil from hell and no telling what else. And Mark had had a big bust up with Monica and demanded his money back and his high-school ring, and then he had gone around to other members of the circle and warned them that they would go to Hell if they didn't get away from Monica.

It seemed there was also something about Monica's embrace that bothered Mark. He thought Tonya's interest in him had fallen off quite a bit. He and Tonya were now separated, and Mark blamed Monica for it. And the worst of this had happened only two weeks before Monica did her "migration."

Well now! Wasn't that interesting! It gave me something to chew over for quite a while. To think of that poor Mosene Taybrook—such a dear woman! And bless Patsy, her little Monica turned out to be a channel of the third power!

You would think that Monica, being married to Douglass Gaulton, could have as much money as she would ever need. But here she was conning these young people out of their valuables. Now wasn't that strange? It struck me that I ought to look into the matter.

There is a little place on Division Street where Eddie Bricker fixes watches and clocks. Eddie and I are good friends on account of Grandfather Gardner's Seth Thomas clock that gets tired every once in a while and has to have its "youth renewed like the eagle's."

The other thing that Eddie does is to buy gold and silver. So I figured he might know whether Monica was selling the stuff that those young people were giving her.

"Has it stopped again?" That is what Eddie said the minute he saw me.

"I am not here about the clock," I said. "Did you know Monica Gaulton?"

"That's Monica Taybrook you're talking about. Sure I knew her, went to high school with her."

I looked at him, and he looked at me.

"Now, you are going to tell me the truth?" I said.

"Of course."

"Did she ever come in here with old gold or old silver to sell?"

"How did you know?"

"Never mind. Just tell me."

"Well, yes. It must have been in August or maybe September. She came in here and told me a tale. Said she had been going through some drawers and had found some old jewelry. Could I give her something for it?

"All right, she opened her purse and pulled out a handkerchief; and when she opened it up, there were about seven or eight rings and a few chains.

" 'How much will you give me for these?' " she asked.

"So I looked at them. One or two were just gold-filled and worthless. But there was about five hundred dollars' worth of metal there. The stones were probably worth something, but they weren't diamonds and rubies.

"Well, there was one class ring—great big thing. And on it, it said, 'John Taliaferro High, 1985.'

"Now she didn't find that in a drawer upstairs at Gaulton's.

"Mrs. Bushrow, I don't fence stolen goods. But at the same time I couldn't accuse Mrs. Douglass Gaulton of possessing stolen property. I didn't know how she got that stuff, and I didn't want to know. I just keep my own nose clean.

"Anyhow, I said to her, 'Look here Monica, I run my place legal. Take your stuff somewhere else.'

"Mad? You bet she was.

"Was I implying that she had stolen those things?

" 'Nope,' I said, 'Just not going to have anything to do with it.' And that was that."

So she hadn't been able to unload those things on Eddie, but there was the fact. Monica had been selling that stuff she was getting from those young people.

"Well, if she couldn't sell it to you," I said, "is there some place where she could?"

Eddie wanted to know why I was so interested. I kind of smiled in a sly way and told him not to bother about that, I was just asking for information.

So he told me about this other place way on down the street, almost to the highway. And then he told me the names of some places in Cooksport. But he said that the people there wouldn't tell me anything. If I really was tracing stolen goods, I should go to the police. So I let it drop at that.

There was one other thing I did about this time.

You remember I said that one of the numbers in Monica's memorandum book was for Dorothy's Beauty Shoppe. I don't ordinarily go to Dorothy, but considering everything, I decided to go over there to have my hair washed. And, yes, Dorothy knew that Monica went off very once in a while—some place near Gatlinburg—she went there for high-stake gambling.

Was she a compulsive gambler and getting all that money from her magic circle so she could satisfy her urge? Or was she gambling because she needed money on short notice? I would have to find a way to look into that.

While I was doing all of this, I just wondered if I was getting any closer to a solution.

Well, maybe so! There was that hint that possibly Monica had left Vegas so she could get away from some mysterious person who made an unexpected appearance. And that would be tied in with what Henry Delaporte had said about criminals and mobsters and so on out there in Vegas.

Then there was all that about Mark Satterwhite shaking off Monica's influence and going to the opposite extreme. If that boy really thought he was Devil-possessed, he might have been desperate enough to doctor Monica's whiskey with a little cyanide. But can you kill the Devil with cyanide? It would be very beneficial if you could.

I know you have heard people say, "To know all is to forgive all." I was getting to know quite a lot about Monica Gaulton, but I had no notion of forgiving her, at least not any time soon.

I couldn't forgive Monica for marrying poor Doug Gaulton. And it would be right hard to forgive her for hoodwinking those young people and getting them to dance around in the moonlight with her. And she stole that car from the rental agency in Las Vegas. Then there was what she did about Virginia's furniture. If it all came out, there would probably be a lot more. And all of those things were bad.

So I couldn't forgive her just then. But I could understand. I just thank the Lord that my life never went in that direction.

XVII

Counting the Silver

JANET GAULTON

"Count the silver?" I said. "Why, no, I haven't thought to count the silver."

It was Mrs. Bushrow on the phone. It did not surprise me that she was working on our case, but it did surprise me that she was calling me to ask if I had counted Big Dad's silver since we were relieved of Monica's company. It had not occurred to me to count the silver.

"She has been selling old gold," Mrs. B. informed me, "and I think you had better count Iris's silver."

Iris, of course, was my husband's grandmother, and in Harriet Bushrow's eyes the silver would always belong to Iris no matter into whose hands it might pass.

When Bill's grandfather went to Florida for the first winter after Iris died, we brought all the silver to our house and put it in the attic. When he came back and opened his house again, we kept the rather extensive tea and coffee service here. We also kept the candelabra and other large pieces. All told, there is at this moment a small fortune in silver in our attic; but the flat silver went back to the big house. The Gaultons were not the kind of people to eat with stainless steel.

So there should be two sets of sterling flatware—the everyday and the company silver. And there had been three or four loving cups, collected here and there, that were returned to the house because—well, because they were objects that meant a lot to Big Dad. But, as we had increasing trouble retaining housekeepers, and as Big Dad began to be—I'll simply say "less responsible"—it seemed best to bring those one by one to our house and put them in the attic with the rest of the trove. Big Dad never seemed conscious of their removal.

But there should still be two services for twelve in Big Dad's house. At least they were there before Big Dad married Monica.

Iris had kept the "company" silver in a chest on the sideboard in the dining room. The chest was kept there still. I would have known if it had been removed. When I opened it, however, it was empty.

It had been a very extensive set of silver—all that you would expect and much more—things like oyster forks, grapefruit spoons, salts and peppers—and all of it heavy silver.

I called to Mrs. Greene, who came down immediately. She did not know anything about it.

Together we went through the kitchen into the pantry where the everyday silver was normally kept. The silver and its chest—the whole thing gone!

"What on earth have you been using for silver all this time?" I demanded.

Poor Mrs. Greene! I am afraid I spoke roughly. I certainly didn't mean to accuse her. She had been harried enough by the police, who had been interrogating us all repeatedly. If under such difficult circumstances she had quit the job, I could not have blamed her. On the other hand, my life and Bill's would be even more complicated if even one of the nurses left us, and the thought that all three might go was my idea of the ultimate nightmare.

Mrs. Greene reported that at some time in August

Monica had explained to her that there was no sense in using silver for everyday purposes and that she had bought a set of stainless. Mrs. Greene had thought this a very reasonable move, as indeed it was, and had seen nothing suspicious in it.

Mrs. Greene and I looked high and low, on the chance that Monica might have hidden the services for safekeeping. We found nothing.

Well, it was insured. That was a comfort.

When I got home I called and reported our findings—or rather, our lack of findings—to Mrs. Bushrow. She was not at all surprised.

I said something about the insurance.

"I hate to tell you," she replied, "but it's beans to doughnuts you will never get a cent out of the insurance company."

"Why?" I asked.

"Unless you can prove there was an intruder or that one of the nurses took it, the only person who could be responsible was Monica. And she was Mrs. Douglas Gaulton."

Of course!

How could there have been an intruder? Since Big Dad's stroke, someone had been alert in that house every minute of the day and night. And even though the night nurse may have dozed, there was in the sickroom, nevertheless, a light, subdued but visible through the windows. It would have been very risky for anyone who was not supposed to be there to get into that house.

"And then, of course," Mrs. Bushrow added, "it would be easy for the insurance company to find the place where Monica sold all that stuff. It would be perfectly legal, you know."

And I suppose it would. Bill has his grandfather's power of attorney, but whether that would prevent Big Dad's legally married wife from selling household goods, I could not say. It was exactly like the sale of the living room furniture.

I was so outraged that Monica should have sold the family silver that I said a few things that I should not have. We have been constantly under suspicion by the police and probably by the community at large. It was all very wearing, and I had been very careful not to talk about it to anyone.

I won't say that Mrs. Bushrow wormed it out of me. But she made it very easy for me to tell her everything I knew—about how we first came to hire Monica to keep house, what the police had found in the will she hoodwinked Big Dad into making in her favor, about how Bill had to use the power of attorney to keep her from spending every cent the poor old man had. I even told Harriet about the dirty trick Monica played on Uncle Norman and Uncle Conrad back in 1952. I shouldn't have said all those things.

But confidence begets confidence, and Mrs. Bushrow told me the things that she knew about the case—about what she had learned from old Mrs. Gifford—the New Agers with whom Monica had been palling around—and the mysterious man Mrs. Gifford had seen go into Big Dad's house the very morning of the day that Monica was poisoned.

And after all, Mrs. Bushrow's reputation for getting at the truth in matters of that kind elicited my confidence. From that point on, the Gaulton family as a whole began to look to her as someone who through her observations and common sense could find the root of the mystery and free us from the horrible suspicion.

By this time it was really getting to us—'specially to Nathan, whose grades had taken a nosedive. I asked him if his schoolmates talked about our little sensation. "Some," he admitted. But I was inclined to think that it might be a great deal. It was so wretchedly unfair for a child to have to put up with whispers and perhaps even taunts.

This thing had now hung over us for more than two months. How I longed for it to be over!

XVIII

Roulette in Gatlinburg

VIRGINIA PETTITOE

You have to understand that I have known Harriet all my life. She and Mother were the very best of friends. We lived in a big house, and she lived in a little house, but otherwise they were as alike as two pennies.

I know now that both Mother and Harriet were women of independent thought and governed their behavior according to codes that were, for them, elastic enough to see them through any necessity. But when I was young, I thought them very sheltered, almost stuffy. I know better now, but it was a bit hard to see their point of view then.

I never dared to call Mrs. Bushrow "Harriet" in my mother's hearing, though of course the name was a household word with us.

Well, I had seen Harriet at the funeral, though nothing passed between us there. The undertaker pushed the family out into the limousine, and off we went to the cemetery.

I will state upfront that I never liked Monica Taybrook, even before she pulled that dirty trick on Norman—and yes, on Conrad, too. She and I were the same age, and until I went to Salem to prep, we were in the same grade. I have never known anyone as hateful as Monica was.

I remember one time when I had a new box of crayons

and Monica broke every one of them. No, I didn't see her do it. But I knew just the same.

I suppose she did it because Mother had Mrs. Taybrook make all my dresses—though of course Mrs. Taybrook made Monica's clothes as well and they were beautiful. But still, my clothes were as pretty as Monica's and similar. That put us in an unnatural comparison. Monica must have been awfully jealous. Perhaps without knowing it, I gave her cause to be that way.

Though I know that the spite and jealousy of childhood and youth should be discarded when we mature, there remained that thing about Norman; so you can imagine how I felt when she came back into our lives and did what she did to Dad. While she was just the housekeeper, I don't suppose I minded it so much. On the other hand, perhaps from her point of view that threw us into competition again.

When she married Dad, I didn't think I could bring myself to speak to her.

I can't blame my nephew Bill. He was my big brother's son and runs the business very smoothly, and he and Jan had always taken the best possible care of Dad. What Bill and Jan did, they did for the best. The whole point of having a housekeeper was to keep Dad in his home and delegate a little of the responsibility. And I was in favor of that. I did not want to see my father become just another inhabitant of a retirement home.

But Monica saw her chance and took it. And the rest was downhill for us.

Harriet Bushrow called me about the first week in this past January.

"Virginia?" I knew who it was the moment she spoke.

"Yes?"

"Hattie Bushrow."

"Yes, Mrs. Bushrow."

"Darling, I wanted to speak to you so bad there at the

funeral, but I just didn't feel like going way out there to the cemetery."

Now, that was transparent, because I already knew that she went to see Dad while we were presenting a united family front at the graveside. She did not want to speak to me then. But now if she was calling me here in Knoxville from her home in Borderville, that meant she had something special on her mind.

"I understand," I said.

"I can imagine how it was for you." She was talking about the charade we had put on at Monica's funeral.

With the preliminaries over, she explained what she wanted. She had found out somehow that Monica had made a mysterious visit to Gatlinburg. She was convinced that Monica had gone there to a gambling den and wanted me to investigate.

Investigate! Me!

"Why?" I asked.

"Well, don't we want to know who the murderer is?"

"What for?" I said.

"Now, honey, you know what for. Don't talk to me like that."

To tell the truth, I would have given anything to know who killed Monica, so we could get the police off our backs and let the Gaulton family return to normal.

"If I knew who the killer was, I would give him a reward," I said.

"I don't know that I can blame you," Harriet agreed before adding, "but poisoning is mighty dirty business, don't you think?"

I suppose she had something there. Yet the idea that I could go sleuthing around Gatlinburg to find a blackjack game in the back room of a third-rate club didn't appeal to me.

I told Harriet, Nothing doing.

"I know where your mother's living room furniture is," Harriet said.

She wanted me to go to this gambling place in return for the name of the gallery in New York that had my furniture. She even knew how much I would have to pay to get it back. We sparred a bit before I gave in. In the end, you see, I was no match for her.

And, of course, if a mysterious visit of Monica's to Gatlinburg helped to explain this wretched mystery, it would be better if I did as she had asked.

Harriet had got her information at a beauty parlor, and it was very sketchy; but, as she pointed out, it would be unlikely that Monica, the kind she was, would be interested in slot machines or bingo. She would crave something more spectacular—like chemin de fer or roulette. And there could hardly be more than one place that offered that sort of play in Gatlinburg.

"You can do it, darling," she insisted. "Just ask around among your friends."

My connections with the underworld are like duck teeth. How I could learn anything about gambling dens in the Smoky Mountains, I did not know.

I spent the rest of the day mulling it over before I thought of Margery Pitman's brother, Ned. Ned Bruster is a bachelor of means who dabbles in small businesses of one kind and another—never in the same thing more than five or six years—seems to come out ahead in everything he takes up. I knew that he was very tweedy, squired glamourous women to the races and in consequence got his picture on the society page rather frequently, and would know about the stylish side of gambling in the region, if there was any.

When he returned my call, it was with "Hello, sweetheart."

I explained my predicament.

"No trouble at all," he said. "Monica Taybrook—the woman who married your father—what was she like?" I described her.

"I take it, then, she was a rather hot item," he observed.

"That's accurate enough," I said. "The police are worrying us to death about her. And if there is anything down here that might divert their attention, what a relief it would be!"

He thought about it a second or two.

"I can think of two possibilities," he said, "but it won't help you."

"Why?" I asked.

"Do you think a croupier is going to be happy about helping the police?" Of course not. Why hadn't I thought of that? But then perhaps that was not what Harriet had had in mind. She wanted the information for purposes of her own. And as I thought of it, I saw with horror what she expected. She expected *me* to go to the place—me—girl detective Virginia Pettitoe; and I was supposed to prowl the underworld and bring back the incriminating information.

"Look," I told Ned, "if you could just find out where Monica went, maybe I could go up there and at least look around."

"Fair enough. I'll get back to you."

A little over a week later he called again and said, "I have found the place. It's in Gatlinburg, but I'll have to go with you or you will never get in."

I had to smile at the stunning couple we would make. "Mr. Ned Bruster and Glamourous Widow Together at Casino." What a headline that would be! I thought of Harriet Bushrow as she was in her heyday. Bless her old heart. Ned should be escorting someone like her. It would be a lot more fun for him.

I did my best to look like a big spender. I have a teal blue cocktail dress and an evening bag with lots of sparkle to it. That and as much gold jewelry as I could muster went as far as possible to make me look authentic.

Ned is really a sweet man. He's more than that: he is a delight. We talked so naturally and pleasantly that the ride to Gatlinburg was over before I wanted it to be.

It would not be wise to describe the location of the casino, if that is what it can be called. All I can say is that we drove around many curves and up and down several hills before we passed through a very ordinary-looking gate into a thick grove which sheltered a large old house.

There was a graveled parking lot. As I got out of the car I could hear music muted through large windows, beyond which people were dining. The place was not elegant or even attractive—red brick in no particular style, common-sensical and solid although slightly down at the heels.

"We'll be expected to eat first," Ned was saying. "I think that's the best way. Then when the maître d' comes and asks us if we would like something else, we'll tell him we might like to go upstairs."

It sounded very exciting and just a shade wicked. I was glad I had an experienced escort. I felt perfect safe with him.

It happened just as Ned had predicted. After we had dined, the maître d' came to our table, Ned made his speech, and we were shown to a large room on the second floor. I suppose it had once been a master bedroom.

Heavy drapes covered the windows. The wallpaper was a deep red, which didn't blend with my teal blue dress at all. And there were some metal chairs—aluminum I would think, with gray vinyl seats. The carpet was green with a pattern of swirling leaves.

There were two gambling tables in the room, only one of them in use just then. It was roulette, and six or seven people were playing.

Ned explained everything to me and bought me chips so could play. The beautiful thing about roulette is that you don't have to have a brain to take part.

I rather enjoyed it.

After I had won a little and lost a little, several people left the table, and the croupier excused himself for a moment—no doubt to use the rest room. When he came back, I said, "A friend of mine, I believe, used to play here."

The man looked at me in a blank sort of way that said, "No concern of mine."

"Monica Gaulton," I said.

"Oh, Monica!"

"Yes, I went to school with her." I wasn't about to explain any closer relationship.

"We read about her."

"Yes, poor dear!"

"Unlucky woman," the croupier observed.

"Yes, she was . . . Oh, but you mean here at the table!"

"Lost twenty thousand dollars in one night," he muttered.

"When was that?" I asked.

He looked up at one corner of the room and thought a moment. "Actually," he said, "it couldn't have more than a day or two before we read in the paper that she was dead."

That damned woman had gambled away every cent she had got by selling my chairs!

I thought I had better not press my luck any further either at the table or in my questioning of the croupier. I told Ned I thought I had had enough play for one night, and we departed.

XIX

One Brown Fender

HARRIET GARDNER BUSHROW

I declare, it was enough to drive a woman crazy to try to figure out how that poison got into Monica's whiskey. Just about anybody could have put it there. That woman had been into enough mischief with enough folks to make a good-sized Fourth of July picnic.

You know they say if you want to find the scoundrel who did the deed, you had better follow the money trail. So I thought I would just try that.

Of course, we all need money; and Monica obviously learned that lesson early in life, what with her little mother pushing her toward the kind of life that requires more money than Mosene Taybrook ever dreamed of. And that meant that Monica would be scrambling for it until the day she died. Mosene didn't think about that, did she?

So Monica seduced those two Gaulton boys—nothing in the world but a money proposition, which naturally caused the police to suspect Norman and Conrad. Well, that was the money that got Monica to New York.

We don't know much about Monica's finances while she was in New York; but that friend of hers, that Tina out in Las Vegas, said Monica had lots of money when Tina first knew her. And then she lost it and kept throwing everything she could scrape together into the chance of winning at those games and so on.

Now when somebody does that, either she has the habit or there is some special reason why she has to have a sight of money.

And next, she stole a car and sold it. Now, with all the things I know about Monica Taybrook, I don't think she would do anything that risky if she hadn't absolutely had to. Well the car brought her here; and when she sold it, that gave her enough money to move into a little apartment just down the street from Doug Gaulton.

All right, she had to have money to live. And that was why she hired herself out as a housekeeper to Doug Gaulton; and that would have been perfectly honest and honorable if she hadn't snookered poor Doug into marriage. You would think she would be satisfied with that.

It is easy to understand Monica's maneuvers up to a certain point. Monica was not dumb. She could expect poor Doug to die any minute—'specially after he had his stroke—and that would leave Monica with millions. But somewhere along in there things began to happen that I didn't understand. Why did she have to do all those cheap, undignified things like stealing Virginia's furniture and cheating those young people out of their jewelry and so on for a few thousand when she had an easy life for the present and riches waiting for her in the future?

There had to be an answer to that, if I could only find it. Then perhaps the rest of the mystery, like morning mists in the valleys, would clear up and we would see the reason for everything.

Now let's back up just a little. Do you remember that Tina, the girl in Vegas, said that Monica was out there for a while and then left suddenly and didn't come back for a long time—and she never told anyone why she disappeared in such a hurry? And then, do you remember how Edna Finch down at the Cup and Saucer reported that somebody came into the restaurant one day and Monica turned into a scared rabbit and wouldn't come out of the kitchen until the man was gone? And of course Olive Gifford saw that car with one brown fender and the man who looked like a possum. Can you add all that up?

Well *I* added it up, several times, and unfortunately I got different answers. Of course the items in my little exercise were very iffy, which no doubt contributed to the variety of possible conclusions.

For example, I could have been wrong about the man. He could have been somebody looking for yardwork—wanting to clean out the guttering or paint the garage doors. You know how those people make you feel like you have the shabbiest place in the neighborhood. Was it a man like that with his one brown fender?

Maybe not. Maybe he was sent by the mob with—I think they call it a contract. I remembered what Henry Delaporte said about all those gangsters out in Las Vegas. If Monica did the kind of stunt out there that she did in Borderville, it wouldn't be hard to imagine that she had stirred up a hornet's nest. But Henry also pointed out that the Mafia travels in style. They are not the sort of people to drive around with one brown fender.

The man with one brown fender could very well be just a poor old fellow; and yet somebody from that rank of life might have as much reason to kill Monica as anybody else. Maybe he was hired to kill Monica. I would think a man would have to need the money really bad before he would take a risk like that.

So let's suppose somebody paid him to kill Monica. Who would that be? No doubt somebody that suffered from some of Monica's crooked doings. But Monica must not have been afraid of him, because she told Mrs. Greene not to come in until ten o'clock so that she could be alone with him. And that looked like there was a secret—maybe an uncomfortable secret—between Monica and the man with the brown fender.

But—and this is really weird—the way Olive reacted to the man, you would think there might be something sexual about the visit. I couldn't believe that for one minute. Monica had far too much style and pride. She would have been more picky about the man—unless money was involved. She could pull off a sham like marrying a poor old fellow with one foot in the grave if that made her Mrs. Douglass Gaulton—successor to Iris Gaulton—and, at the same time, rich! Otherwise she would surely have hunted up somebody with a lot more spizerinktum.

And so, I come back to that shabby man with one brown fender—what could he possibly be to Monica Gaulton?

On the other hand, there is another far-off shaky possibility. Could Monica's death be a case of suicide—caused, maybe, by the arrival of the mysterious man with the brown fender?

At first I just threw that thought away. Survival was the big idea for the Monica Taybrook I knew. There was nothing weak about that gal. Her idea was to push everybody out of her way and climb right over those who objected. She wasn't the type who would kill herself—not Monica!

And yet the Monica I knew would rather die than take second place. She had always had her eye on the main chance, and all her prospects were looking up because she was going to get all of Doug's money, the house, the business, and everything. Still, if by her various shenanigans she had got into something we didn't know about—something from which she couldn't get away—and things were going to cave in on her—in a case like that, if she could pass off the scene in a spectacular way, she might prefer it.

They tell me cyanide is quick. So that part of it might

have appealed to her. And just think. There isn't a more spectacular way to die than to be poisoned from a drink of whiskey while wearing a gentleman's full-dress suit before a fashion show at First Presbyterian Church.

Besides, it would look like murder. And the likely suspects would be her in-laws. Can't you just see Monica Taybrook laughing from the other side, at the Gaultons trying to find alibis and all that?

So if you take the suicide idea from that angle, maybe that would appeal to Monica. In the book about the Rotary Club mystery, the murder was made to look like a suicide. Why couldn't this case be just the opposite?

Well, I just teetered one way and another. The whole thing was such a puzzle.

In the second week in January something happened that brought the man with the brown fender more into the picture. That was the week when Ella Sue Huey died and was to be buried from the Guthrie Funeral Home in Cooksport.

Ella Sue was—like me—just about the last of her family. All the folks she had left were the children of a third cousin, and they still lived on the old Huey place just over the Virginia line about five miles from Cooksport.

Well, they wanted to bury Ella Sue from Cooksport because that was convenient for them. They never gave a thought to the fact that Ella Sue lived for seventy-five years right here in Borderville. And all of her friends—and there are not many of us left—are up in years; and most of them won't poke their noses out in weather like what we expect in January.

So the upshot of that was that Sarah Dogget's niece offered to take her car and drive some of the ladies in Ella Sue's Sunday School class over to Cooksport.

I would have been happy to take them in my car; but since Sarah called me before I could think about it, I said I would be delighted to go with the others. And that's what happened.

It is a very pretty drive to Cooksport. After you get out of town, you go over a hill and then the highway goes along the side of a valley where there is a nice little stream tumbling over rocks—just as lovely as you might see in a travel brochure or on a calendar. There are fields and houses along the road and little businesses here and there, and then the knobs go up steep on the other side of the creek. Even in the winter when the leaves are off the trees, the white trunks of the sycamores look so pretty against the dark green pines.

But as I say, there are little businesses here and there along the way.

Now, it is a strange thing to me that on the highway to Parsons City and to Ambrose Courthouse there are no "objectionable" businesses. But on the way to Cooksport there is just one disgrace right after the other. I mean "massage parlors" and "lingerie studios" and things like that.

Well, there is this one place. It is a brick building—not bad looking as business buildings go—in good condition, with gravel spread around in front and on the sides for people to park, and a big sign stretching the full length of the roof that says:

ADULT BOOKS AND FILMS

Sarah saw it and was just incensed. She said, "Don't look. Look the other way!"

I don't know how we could look the other way unless we had already seen it! And I don't know why I should be embarrassed about the *sign*. There is not a dirty word in it. And as I say, the building is not an eyesore. There was no reason to blush or look away. So I didn't.

And it was a good thing I looked. For there at the side of the building facing the highway was an old blue car with one brown fender!

I drew in my breath.

Sarah thought I had been scandalized. "It's just too bad that they allow such things," she said, and I let it go at that.

But I wasn't about to let that car with a brown fender slip my mind. No, indeed, I hardly heard a word the minister—a young man from the Beaver Fork Community Church—said. And all the way up to the Hueys' little family cemetery, my mind was still on that blue car with the one brown fender. Oh, I said all the right things—told the third cousin's daughter what a sweet service it was, shook hands with the young minister, just a nice little country fellow. I did all that with my mind on *an adult book store!*

On the way back to Borderville I made it a point to see if the car was still there. It was almost five o'clock then. And there it was, all right.

That meant that my man—if he was my man—had been in there almost three hours. Either he had a strong taste for dirty books or he was an employee of the store.

Well, what could I do about it? I couldn't say to Sarah's niece, "Stop! I want to go into that adult book store." There would have been three cases of heart failure right there in the car. You can imagine what I felt, for I thought I had lost my best chance to find the key to the mystery.

I couldn't get my mind off of it all evening. I dratted Sarah's niece. If it hadn't been for her, I would have been in my own car and could have done as I pleased. But then, I probably would have had the other Sunday School ladies with me anyhow. It would have turned out the same.

I decided the thing to do was drive out there the next day and see what I would find.

Anybody who knows me knows that I wouldn't have had the slightest hesitation about going into such a place if it suited me to do so. But there was a problem about that.

136

How could I convince the people inside that I was a customer—a woman ninety years old! I don't suppose many ninety-year-old women go in for pornography. So I had to think of a plan.

Lamar had a nice pair of field glasses. I could take the glasses and find a good place to park and observe. And then I thought it might be a good thing to get a picture of the man if he came out of the shop. So I got out Lamar's camera and sort of refreshed my mind about how to use it and got some film and had the young lady at the store put it in the camera for me so that I wouldn't do it wrong.

It was a perfect day—nippy—but the sun was bright; and I figured that if I dressed warmly and parked in the sun, I would be just as comfortable in my car as I would be in my own living room. And then about three o'clock that afternoon, I went out on the Cooksport highway where that "adult" book store is.

And sure enough, there was that same old car with its one brown fender parked in the same place. So that proved that the man who owned the car was employed by the bookstore.

I drove on down the road until I could turn around.

As I had passed the bookstore I had glanced at what was on the other side of the highway. It was a place where I could pull my car off the road and back up behind some sparse bushes and sit and keep an eye out for my suspect the way we did in the DAR mystery.

It would have been nice if I could have got the man's license number. But the car was parked with the front toward the highway; and since there are no license plates for the fronts of cars in Tennessee, I would have had to get out of my car and walk around to the back of the other car to see the number. If I had done that, the man would have seen me sure as fate.

I got my car about half hidden behind the bushes and possessed my soul in patience. I was sitting pretty, just waiting for the man to come out.

Well, I had my field glasses all adjusted, and I had my camera on the seat beside me ready to take the man's picture, though there was no telling when that would happen. I thought I had all the time in the world.

The sun was on the car, and it was so comfortable and warm there, and other cars just kept going by and going by. Time kept passing too, and I found it hard to keep my mind on the bookstore.

Once in a while a car would stop and someone would go in. And of course I would use the field glasses when they came out, in case one of them was the man.

As I say, it was warm in the car and the traffic kept going by and going by, and I must have dozed off.

I woke with a start and here was a rough old fellow right at my window.

"What do you think you are doing here, lady?"

At first I could hardly gather my wits.

He knocked on the window, and I turned the key in the ignition so I could put the window down a crack—but not much—and talk to him.

"I beg your pardon," I said.

"I said, 'What the hell do you think you are doing here?' " He was really talking loud.

The field glasses and the camera were right there where he couldn't help seeing them. I gulped two or three times and looked around to the other side.

"Why, I was just . . . I was just. . . . Well I am with the environmental people. I am observing."

"Observing what?"

Well, thank the Lord, from that spot, way, way off down by the river I could see the paper factory. People are always complaining about how it pollutes. Of course I don't know whether it does or not. But that's neither here nor there.

"I am observing the paper factory," I said. "For the Environmental Association." I just put as much authority into my voice as I could, and ice cream wouldn't have melted in my mouth.

But it didn't have any effect on the man except that he took his eye off of me for a second and seemed surprised that you actually could see the factory from that spot.

Then he said: "Well, this is private property. There is no parking allowed here."

My, he did sound gruff!

"Oh, I'm so sorry. I didn't know."

Of course it was private property. Most property is private, but I knew very well it was not *his* private property. This man just might be the man I had been looking for. I couldn't just put the camera up in his face and take his picture. But I could mark his features very closely so I would never forget.

He had black greasy hair with just a little gray; brown eyes—mean eyes, but that might have been just the mood he was in; kind of a loose mouth with bad teeth—dirty, tobacco-stained and with one of the uppers broken; long nose, wide forehead. You *might* say he looked a little like a possum. He was leaning over to talk to me through the car window, so I really couldn't be sure how tall he was, but I guessed he was a little above medium height.

"I'm telling you to get off this property and don't come back," he said.

I gave him a mild blank look that said nothing but seemed to annoy him.

I said, "I am sorry if I have damaged your property," and pressed the button to put the window up. Then I started the car and just went bouncing down into the ditch and up onto the highway. I imagine he had to scramble to keep his toes from being run over.

Cars were coming and going on that highway, and the way I came out onto the road caused the car coming up over the hill to put on his brakes. I am sure it was quite a show.

After I got home, I thought, *You fool! You don't know what kind of danger you might have run into out there.* But it was what I deserved. I had gone out there thinking that the man was probably the murderer. It was the greatest likelihood that he would object in the strongest possible way to me and what I was doing.

All my life I have done things that weren't safe at all. I think it all comes from the way my father spoiled me and let me do whatever I wanted to do. I had no fear, and it drove my poor mother crazy. I remember when I was four years old, I ducked under the rope at the circus and went right up to the elephant. Ma just knew I was going to be trampled.

But to get back to my afternoon's adventure. Suppose this really was the man Olive had seen go in the back door of the Gaulton house the morning Monica died. Olive had made it clear that he was not a proper kind of person for Monica to be receiving as a guest. If by any chance this old man at the adult book store was the same as the old possum that Olive saw, I would have to agree that he wasn't what you would expect on the guest list at Two-O-One Anderson Avenue. This man hadn't gone into the house with Monica to see about fixing the furnace or anything like that, because that wasn't his kind of work. Whatever reason he might have had for being there, it wasn't anything good.

And yet I hadn't got myself very far. I didn't know his name. I didn't have his license number. I didn't have his picture. I didn't even know that he was the same man.

But I had it fixed in my mind that that fellow might somehow be the key to our Music Club mystery. Anybody who got that fussed by an old lady parked opposite his place of business—even if he saw her looking at him with field glasses—was like the wicked that flee when no man pursueth.

And now that he knew me and knew I was watching, any detecting I might do in his direction later on would have to be done without his knowing it. *Very well,* I thought to myself, *I'll drive out there tomorrow and see how he parks his car. If he parks it with the rear toward the road, I'll get his license number.*

It was a little after five o'clock when I got there; and do you know, the car wasn't there. Then I happened to think that five was probably when he got off from work.

The following day, I drove out toward Cooksport again, this time about three o'clock. The car was there, but parked the same way it had been before.

How was I going to handle this? Should I take it to the police? They wouldn't pay any attention to me. One old lady tells another old lady about a car with a mismatched fender. Then the second old lady finds a car with a mismatched fender in a place ten miles away and jumps to the conclusion it is the same car? Did the second old lady see the first car? No. Then how does she know the first car and the second car are the same?

I thought once I might ask Mr. Delaporte to go out there. It wouldn't be quite as suspicious for him to go into that place as it would be for me to do so. But it wouldn't do for him to be seen entering a place like that. I don't mind risking my own reputation. It has enough dents in it already. But Henry Delaporte is one of our leading attorneys. Suppose he wanted to run for office sometime and somebody had seen him coming out of an adult book store.

Drat the state of Tennessee! Why couldn't it put license plates on the front of cars like other self-respecting states! I finally concluded I would just have to lie in wait for the man somewhere near that bookshop and, when he came out, get behind him in traffic and take down his number.

If he got off from work, let's say, at five, why couldn't I park my car on down the road where it couldn't be seen, wait for him to pass, and then follow him? I could see where he went and I would have both his license number and his address.

Unfortunately, my car is all wrong for doing any kind of detective work. It is the car the Rotarians gave me when I solved their mystery. It's a beautiful color—kind of a golden shade. But the trouble is that it is so obvious and easy to spot—as easy as an old blue car with one brown fender would be.

So I would have to be careful. But I believed I could do it.

Some people are going to say I have more sense in my pocket than I have in my head—and that's not much. But the way I had been going wasn't getting me anywhere with this mystery. If the man with the brown fender hadn't poisoned Monica, he certainly had been in the house and was bound to have seen something when he visited Monica on that Saturday. So he had to be an important part of the mystery, and I had to know about him.

All right. The next afternoon—it was a Thursday—I went out on the Cooksport highway and found a side road where I could park just before getting to that adult book store. There I sat until six o'clock, watching every car that went by.

No blue car with a brown fender!

It was disappointing, but I was determined to try it again. This time I would park on the other side of the adult book store.

On Friday I went back out on the highway to watch for the man's car again. I parked on a little crossroad on the Cooksport side of the bookstore, and, sure enough, about five minutes past five, here came the little blue car with its brown fender.

I let him get past me so that there was a car between me and him. Then I followed him almost to the other side of Cooksport.

It was all I could do to stay on his tail. I could have read his license number if I had been close enough. But staying back, that way, I didn't even have a chance.

Well, as he drove on through Cooksport, I began to wonder how far from home I was going to be when he stopped. At last he turned left and drove for about a half mile until he came to a right good-sized building that sat back from the road and had a chainlink fence around it. He turned in there.

There were just a few cars in the parking lot and a light or two in the building. No doubt the people who worked there had just got off and had gone home. About that time an illuminated sign went on up above, and I saw that it was Cooksport Printing and Engraving.

Cooksport Printing and Engraving is one of our big industries. They do all kinds of fine work, and I understand that they print—oh, ever so much of the stock certificates for big companies.

I imagine with all those stock certificates they have to be very careful about security and things like that. Anyhow, I saw that there was a guard at the entrance.

My man, the one I had been following, got out of his old car, walked over to the entrance, showed something to the guard, and walked in.

Eureka, I thought. This is the time for me to get the man's license number. So I pulled into the parking lot and got up close behind his car. I was fishing around in my bag for my memorandum book and was about to take down the number when the guard came over and wanted to know what I was doing. I said I was just turning around. When you say you are going to turn around, you have to do it. And that is why I didn't get the number.

It was a disappointment. But I had learned something. It looked like the man with the old car was working at two jobs: one at that pornography place, and the other at Cooksport Printing and Engraving.

Now you know that unless the man owned the place, running a pornographic bookstore wouldn't have much appeal as an occupation. All the money would go to the owner and the employee would get chicken feed.

This man didn't talk as if he had much education and perhaps was just scraping by. And since he went to Cooksport Printing and Engraving after the other employees had left, maybe he was a janitor and swept the place out.

Now what in the world would anyone like that have to do with Monica? I know we all have poor relatives. And no doubt that dear mother of Monica's had a raft of them. But Mosene Taybrook was such a fine little woman—so ambitious and hard-working, bending over that sewing machine all day. I just couldn't picture her people being like this man.

But still, he was working at two jobs; so at least he was industrious.

He could, after all, be a poor relative. Maybe he came begging for help, and Monica, being married to a Gaulton, would be the relative he would come to, though I knew that she was strapped for cash. Experienced as I was with Monica, I didn't think she was scraping up cash as fast as she could just to give it to a poor relation. I had already learned from Virginia Pettitoe that Monica had blown away the furniture money on roulette down at Gatlinburg. So, no matter how kind her heart might have been (which it wasn't), she didn't have anything to give.

After all, if she really was giving him a little money now

and then, or if he only thought she might give him some-thing sometime later, why would he want to kill her?

I began to think I had found the wrong man. I was only depending on Olive's description of the car. Our lower-class people here often drive cars that have had fenders and such replaced with parts from junkyards. Cars like that seem to be everywhere. So I began to worry that I had been wrong about this man from the beginning.

But if this was the wrong man, why was he so upset when he caught me across the road from the adult book place? If the Baptists hadn't been able to shut that store down, did he think an old woman ninety years old could?

I bet I could if I set my mind to it.

Anyhow, the next morning I called on Olive and asked her about the man's car again. It had been almost three months since Monica's death.

Olive wasn't sure now whether it was the right or the left fender, but she still said the car was blue and the fender was brown. No, she hadn't seen the man since, and she knew all the cars that Doug's nurses had. She kept up with what went on at the Gaulton place all right—told me what days Janet brought in groceries. I got the impression that Monica's death had limited the interesting things that Olive could see out of her window. It is strange how the details of a neighborhood take root in a vacant mind!

All the same, I had this feeling that I was somehow closer to the end of my mystery.

XX

A Small Labor Problem

HENRY DELAPORTE

I am not violating a client's confidence in stating that Bill Gaulton came to my office on January 9 of this year. He was beginning the new year right by doing something he should have done long before. For a good many years I had been the attorney for Gaultwood, but up to that point Bill had never consulted me about what we might call his inconveniences with the police. Being completely aware of his own innocence and confident of the innocence of the rest of his family, he was so self-assured that it probably did not cross his mind to retain me in the matter. To him, perhaps, it would have appeared to be admission of weakness to have consulted counsel regarding the interrogation he and his family were undergoing.

No doubt it had been a trying time for him. The police, having no clear leads in the case of Monica Gaulton, had concentrated on the persons who were in a position to profit most by her death. And the most obvious person was Bill Gaulton.

Gaultwood, formerly known as Gaulton Office Furniture, is operated by Gaulton Inc., which is a family corporation formed in 1925 when Douglass Gaulton inherited his father's business. The original stockholders were: Douglass Gaulton with fifty-one percent of the stock; Iris Gaulton, with twenty-five percent; and Iris's father, Conrad Ellison, with twenty-four percent. When Ellison died, he left his shares equally distributed to his four grandchildren. Upon Iris Gaulton's death she left her shares to be divided among her children. Unfortunately, the division did not come out even; and the oldest son, Bill's father, received two more shares than the other heirs did. Then, when Bill, Sr., died, Bill, Jr., received his father's stock. At the present time Douglass Gaulton has fifty-one percent, and Bill has fourteen.

By the will that I drew up for Douglass Gaulton some years before his second marriage, he was leaving his fifty-one percent as follows: eleven percent to Bill, ten percent to Conrad, ten percent to Norman, ten percent to Virginia, and ten percent to Bill's son, Nathan, who is apparently the very apple of the old man's eye. In all testamentary distributions of the stock, a very obvious effort to equalize the legacies was shown through bequeathing other properties to those heirs who had received fewer shares in Gaultwood.

It can be seen then, that Bill and his son, whose shares he would control until the boy comes of age, would have in hand thirty-five percent of Gaultwood, the income from which should be a very comfortable sum. Thus, if Monica had inherited all fifty-one percent of Douglass Gaulton's stock, the biggest loser would be Bill, who would have only the fourteen percent he had received from his father and his grandmother. He would control Nathan's shares; but in light of the ill will between himself and Monica, he would be deprived of the presidency of the company.

Bill had been controlling his grandfather's affairs by means of the power of attorney that Douglass Gaulton had had me draw up so that he could spend his winters in Florida without the routine concerns of his estate. This power, which undoubtedly formed the chief contention between Monica and Bill, would cease upon Douglass Gaulton's death.

It was established that the flask from which Monica had drunk the poisoned whiskey had been habitually kept in a cabinet in the breakfast room of the Gaulton house. Because the poison could have been placed in the flask at any time prior to Mrs. Gaulton's death, it was impossible for any suspect to clear himself or herself through alibi.

The police were thoroughly baffled by the case and returned again and again to the interrogation first of Bill Gaulton, and then of Jan, his wife.

Bill, as I have said, was perfectly confident that no case could be made against himself or his wife. The investigation came to a lull.

Then the police bought the idea that Bill had employed one of the nurses to poison Mrs. Gaulton. They began their investigation of the women in a rather moderate manner. They had interrogated all three of them routinely immediately upon Monica's death. After a month had passed, they returned to that interrogation. The women were perhaps a bit more nervous at this point. Again there was a lapse in the investigation; and when the police returned to the case, their interrogation was very much more intensive.

The women became quite upset, and two of them threatened to quit. How this would improve their condition is not evident; but such a threat to the even tenor of Douglass Gaulton's household was becoming a serious problem for the younger Gaultons.

These were the conditions under which Bill Gaulton retained me to represent, not only himself, but the nurses who were taking care of his grandfather. Bill realized that there was nothing I could do effectively until a charge had been made. But the psychology of being represented by counsel during interrogation had the desired effect on the women and relieved the strain on young Bill and his wife.

On the other hand, the continuation of the mystery suggested even greater stress for the family. If the death of

Monica Gaulton were never explained, suspicion would attach to them forever. It would perhaps not trouble the older generation inasmuch as Mrs. Pettitoe and her brothers lived out of town. But Bill and his wife had no escape. And of course there was the boy. They were forced to remain in a town where rumors never die unless they are scotched by obvious fact.

In unguarded conversation at home I unintentionally aroused the strong sympathies of my wife for the plight of the young Gaultons. The reader may remember that Helen had quite a lot to do with the famous DAR mystery, as did Mrs. Lamar Bushrow, to whom, I fear, my wife communicated the gist of what I have stated here.

Although the facts of the matter have now become common knowledge and were inevitably to have been revealed, clearly I should not have spoken of them to Mrs. Delaporte. But there are some things that cannot be helped.

XXI

Nurse Talk

HARRIET GARDNER BUSHROW

I have gotten to be right friendly with Mrs. Greene. She's the day nurse for Doug Gaulton. She is always very neat and pleasant; and when I visit Doug, since he can't say anything, I do most of my talking with her.

When Helen Delaporte told me that the police were after the nurses again, I decided I ought to call on Doug—and, of course, Mrs. Greene. I hadn't seen them since January, so it was high time I did.

I had a little pot of African violets that were just outdoing themselves; they were the most beautiful orchid shade. There is not much I can do for Doug except bring him something good to eat—custards and things like that—or something to look at. So I took my African violets and went to visit.

I talked to Doug a little while—reminded him of good times we had when Iris and Lamar were still with us. I don't know whether it does him any good or not, but there is not much else I can say.

Then, after I had said as much as I could think of to Doug, I turned to Mrs. Greene.

Every time I come in and talk to Doug, she puts on her reading glasses and sits there with her book open. When I get through with that, she takes off her glasses and puts the book aside. Then she goes downstairs with me and we talk quite a bit before I leave. It is so much nicer to talk about Doug's condition where he can't hear us, for I am sure he follows every word we say.

So when I got downstairs, I said, "Now, I want you to tell me the truth."

She gave a little smile and said, "You know, Mrs. Bushrow, I always try to."

"Well," I said, "I knew Doug and Iris from when I first moved here. And that is over seventy years now. So whatever affects Doug or his family affects me. I want you to explain just what this trouble is that you and the other nurses are having with the police."

Her face changed. All that cheerfulness on the surface was gone. If I ever saw a woman who was troubled, she was that woman.

"Mrs. Bushrow," she began, "I've been on lots of cases. And we try not to get emotional about our patients. But poor Mr. Gaulton! I just don't want to think of leaving him.

"And it isn't me, you know, that the police are so hard on. It's Miss Thorpe and Mrs. Thompson. But I tell you if Bill Gaulton—the nicest fellow that ever was—if Bill hadn't got Mr. Delaporte to sit there with us, I don't know how much longer any of us could have stood it.

"You see, Mrs. Bushrow, the police keep after me to tell what I know about the other two.

"I don't know anything about them. And I wouldn't want to tell if I did. But if I say anything at all, I'm just afraid I am going to get one or the other in trouble.

"Mrs. Bushrow, I'm a Christian woman, and I try to do right. But sometimes I just don't know what to do."

I could see that this thing was getting close to the bone. "What in the world are the police asking about?" I said. "Do they think one of you poisoned Mrs. Gaulton?"

"You would say so if you heard the questions they ask."

"Now look," I said, "you know I don't believe for one minute that you or Mrs. Thompson or Miss Thorpe had anything to do with Monica Gaulton's death. So tell me all about it. Maybe I can help."

Mrs. Greene knew about me and my success in the DAR case and in the Rotary Club mystery. So she knew I wasn't asking just because I am nosy, though I am, and she could trust me to protect anyone who was innocent.

"Well," she said, "the trouble all began because of those young people who started coming here in the evenings for those circles or whatever you call them. It never happened when I was here, thank the Lord, because I have the day shift and they didn't come in the daytime.

"Now, Mrs. Bushrow, I was brought up a Methodist, and I imagine you were brought up pretty much the same way I was. I don't have any faith in that mumbo-jumbo or those circles or crystals or robes or anything like that. But if other people go in for that stuff, it's all right with me.

"But Miss Thorpe, now, she's different. She goes to the Church of God, and they are a lot stricter than the Methodists, and I don't say that is bad. But I think it is going a little far to say that people are Devil-possessed because they do all kinds of things like the stuff that Mrs. Gaulton had here in the house." She paused to catch her breath. But she wasn't through with what she had to say.

"I guess it's all wicked. I *know* it's wicked. It's wicked like a lot of other things that people do every day and never think a thing about it. But *Devil-possessed?*

"I'll have to admit that if I thought they were really Devil-possessed, that would be mighty scary. How do you feel about it?"

I said I had known Monica from a very early time, and I thought she was mean and ungrateful to her mother and she had treated the Gaulton family unspeakably, and that was my idea of Devil possession. But as far as that New Age nonsense goes, that was just *crazy*.

"Oh, don't use that word."

"Why not?"

"That might be worse than 'Devil-possessed.' "

"Why?" I asked, "Do they think one of you is crazy?"

"Miss Thorpe." Mrs. Green nodded her head.

"Miss Thorpe is crazy?"

"I didn't say it. And I never saw her do anything or heard her say anything that I would call crazy—like 'insane'—though all of us do or say something crazy once in a while. But I'll tell you how it happened."

Then she began at the beginning with the first time Miss Thorpe discovered all that about the New Agers and their crystals and their meditations. It was very offensive to Miss Thorpe's beliefs. She spoke often about it to Mrs. Greene in the few minutes while the two women were changing shifts.

Apparently it preyed on Miss Thorpe's mind until finally she confronted Monica with what she had observed. Monica told her to mind her own business.

Because it was a religious thing with Miss Thorpe, she regarded it as very much her business to witness against this evil power.

So the situation got worse and worse. Monica said she was going to fire Miss Thorpe. But Bill wouldn't let her—said to pay no attention to Miss Thorpe, and it would blow over. Then he advised Miss Thorpe to pray for Monica—he had no objection to that—but just leave her alone otherwise.

Well the next thing that Miss Thorpe convinced herself of was that Monica was some form of the Devil or possibly some kind of minion, who was stretching an evil power over the young people who were in the New Age group.

So Miss Thorpe got hold of one of the young men—it

was Mark Satterwhite—and convinced him that he had been Devil-possessed.

When Mrs. Greene got to that part of her story, I realized I had heard about this before. That little Terri Archer had told me that Mark Satterwhite had broken off from the circle and had a row with Monica.

"So that's what happened," I said.

"Oh, that's not all," Mrs. Greene assured me. "Mrs. Gaulton got in a towering rage and said she was going to have Miss Thorpe put in the insane asylum again."

"Again?"

"Yes, Miss Thorpe was in the asylum for six years. Paranoia, you know."

I had had no idea of that.

Mrs. Greene assured me that Miss Thorpe was completely cured, though a little strange. But then most of us have our little quirks.

"No," Mrs. Greene said, "there is nothing wrong with her that way, and she was trying to do good, don't you see."

I thought there was considerable to be said for Miss Thorpe's position on the matter. It wouldn't be at all hard to think there was a devil in Monica.

"But if the police think that maybe Monica was murdered by Miss Thorpe because Monica threatened to send her back to the asylum or maybe just because Miss Thorpe is crazy—if they think that, all of that applies only to Miss Thorpe. Why do the police keep after you and Mrs. Thompson? I don't understand that."

"Oh, no. It isn't just Miss Thorpe. I really think they believe it was Mrs. Thompson who did it."

"Mrs. Thompson?"

"Yes. You see Mrs. Thompson actually threatened Mrs. Gaulton. It was on the Thursday before Mrs. Gaulton was killed. And the worst part about it is that I heard her do it."

Of course, I had to have an explanation of that. It seems

154

that Mrs. Thompson came in a few minutes before four that afternoon and Mrs. Greene heard this awful fuss going on in the kitchen. (The kitchen is right there off the hall— where you come in the back door.) What Mrs. Greene heard was: "If you do, you won't live very long to tell about it."

Now how would you take that? Was it a threat? Or just old-fashioned spite? I bet you've said things like that many a time. I know I have.

Well, Mrs. Greene, like a good citizen, when the police were asking her about everything, told them exactly what she heard. And that is what put the cat among the pigeons.

"But what on earth was Mrs. Thompson so mad about?" I asked.

"About what Mrs. Gaulton said to Miss Thorpe—that she was going to have her put back in the asylum."

"But why did that upset Mrs. Thompson?"

"Oh," Mrs. Greene said, "you don't know?"

"No."

"Mrs. Thompson is Miss Thorpe's sister."

So there I had it. And no wonder the police were investigating Mrs. Thompson and Miss Thorpe. And no wonder Mrs. Greene was in the middle of it. And of course, there was a brand-new motive: Miss Thorpe not wanting to go back to the asylum and her sister protecting her. And if Miss Thorpe did the murder, she would get off on account of insanity. But if Mrs. Thompson did it, she would go to the pen.

And Mrs. Greene would be the chief witness.

XXII

Financial Report

BILL GAULTON

A good while ago I came across a photograph of Mrs. Bush-row standing beside my grandmother. The picture must have been taken over sixty years ago. They looked so young! And they were flappers! It was hard for me to believe that they were ever the age I was when I found the picture.

I cannot remember a time when I did not know Mrs. B. I remember a Thanksgiving afternoon when I was five or six years old. We were all at Big Dad's house. My mother usually brought something for me to play with and occupy my time on such occasions because I had no cousins or siblings with whom to play. But this time she had forgotten the toy. It was raining, and I couldn't go outside. I guess I was fretful and making a disturbance. That was when Mrs. Bush-row came to the rescue.

She said, "Go into the kitchen and ask Lily for a piece of string; and when you come back, I'll show you something."

It was red string. I remember that as clearly as I remember anything, though red string can't have been very common.

I brought it into the living room. Mrs. Bushrow told me to stand in front of her.

She said, "I'm going to show you how to make a cat's cradle."

If you know the cat's cradle, you know that it is never finished. It can go on for any length of time as the string passes back and forth between the participants. If there is such a thing as a story of my life, that episode has to be a vignette.

I go back with Harriet Bushrow as far as I go with anybody. I guess that's why I can't say no when she asks me to do anything.

I had heard rumors from Aunt Virginia and Jan that Mrs. B. was working on the family mystery: Who killed Monica? God knows I wanted that mystery cleared up. The constant repetition of police interrogations, apart from consuming time I could well spend elsewhere, was insulting. It was as if they doubted my word. Consequently, I was not averse at all to helping Mrs. Bushrow in any way that I could. I knew that none of us had poisoned Monica, and I just wanted to clear the mystery away and put the whole thing behind me.

About the second week in January she called me at the office.

"Do you have any way of knowing if there was a specific time when Monica began paying out a lot more money than usual?" she asked.

After the wedding and before Big Dad had his stroke, Monica was one of the all-time big spenders in this town. She bought clothes. One expensive item that I specially remember was a mink coat. And she entertained lavishly at the club—a set that Jan and I did not go with, but apparently they thought Monica was neat.

It wouldn't have been any of my business except that I had power of attorney, mostly to act for Big Dad when he was in Florida in the winter months. The trip Monica and

Big Dad took to Florida the winter after they married was what tipped me off to Monica's extravagance.

During that winter, as I had done before, I collected dividend checks, clipped coupons, etc., and deposited the proceeds in the same account where I had always deposited them before: Douglass B. Gaulton. And of course I got the bank statements that came to the house and examined them closely, as I had been doing before the marriage, because Big Dad had become a trifle erratic about finance.

I was mildly surprised to discover a second Gaulton account—on the face of it, a joint account, but in fact an account used by Monica alone. Big Dad had transferred something like $30,000 into it, which was not unreasonable when you think of expenses of housekeeping such as redecorating, etc., which would be quite legitimate when a bride of whatever age comes into an old house. But just before the two of them left for Florida, Big Dad had transferred $100,000 into the joint account.

Even that might have been reasonable. If Big Dad had had his stroke in Florida instead of here, it would have been most providential to have an ample balance to draw on for things like intensive care, air ambulance, etc.

But when the statement for the first month of the Florida episode came in, I was astonished. They were spending in the neighborhood of $10,000 per week. It was not that Big Dad could not afford that amount. But the Gaulton family has always been conservative in everything.

Shortly after Monica and Big Dad returned home, there was the stroke; and I took over the financial affairs of my grandfather completely. Monica was furious, but she had no option.

I agreed to insure a balance of $1,000 at the beginning of each month in the joint account. I would take care of taxes, doctor's bills, nursing expenses, utilities, and major repairs from the Douglass B. Gaulton account. All she needed to take from the joint account was household and personal expenses.

It was very obviously unpleasant for her—and unpleasant for me as well. I suspected that Big Dad had made a second will, but I did not actually know then that the new will would leave everything to Monica. Under the circumstances, I was merely trying to protect the estate.

Each month, then, from the time that Big Dad had his stroke until last March I kept the balance in the joint account at the agreed level.

Then some peculiar things began to happen. Monica began to overdraw the account. She blamed it on the plumber's bill, which she had paid although that was contrary to our agreement. There were electricians' bills, and a bill for landscaping—she had had the spruce-pines behind the house cut down, and there was an outrageous expense in that. All of this she had paid by check. I would ask for the bills, but she either had some excuse or defied me. Of course I had to cover the checks. There was nothing else I could do.

Relations between myself and my grandfather's wife were never cordial, but they were now at their lowest.

I had reported more or less all of this to the police, and now I reported it to Mrs. Bushrow.

"Does that help you?" I asked.

There was a pause at the other end of the line. "Maybe," she said doubtfully. Then her tone changed. "I just keep stirring in more and more ingredients," she added, "and maybe we'll have something cooking in a little while."

XXIII

An Unexpected Witness

HARRIET GARDNER BUSHROW

This case just didn't seem to be getting anywhere. All the clues were about the dead woman. But the person who put the poison in the flask was like the wind: we knew someone had been there because we saw what had happened.

Was the poison mixed with the whiskey before it was poured into the flask? The police had searched the house and found a half-empty bottle of whiskey, but the whiskey showed no trace of cyanide.

Perhaps the poisoner mixed just enough cyanide cocktail to fill the flask, poured it in, and waited for the rest to happen. But if that was so, Monica would surely think it strange that a flask that was rarely used—I would suppose it was rarely used—would be full of whiskey. And how would the poisoner be sure that Monica would be using the flask and somebody else would not be poisoned by mistake?

If the poisoner placed only the cyanide in the flask, how would he know that Monica would fill the flask and be poisoned?

Now, I believe that Monica was very nervous about that fashion show. She would surely know that every old cat in Borderville had her claws out ready to tear their mistress of ceremonies to shreds. Call it nerves, call it stage fright—I know why Monica needed a nip just before she was going to make her appearance down there at the church. But how did the poisoner know that Monica would use that particular flask?

Or did Miss Thorpe or Mrs. Thompson do it—in order to keep poor Miss Thorpe out of the asylum, as the police were thinking? Or was one of the nurses hired to do it by the Gaulton family or someone else?

Also to be considered was that two-hour period from eight to ten when Mrs. Greene was told not to come to the house. Did someone—the man with the brown fender or someone else—prepare the whiskey on the mere chance that Monica was planning to take it with her to the fashion show? Or did Monica, without knowing it, tell the poisoner that she intended to take the flask with her?

What I needed was a fact—just one fact. If I could get a fact, perhaps the whole puzzle would fall into place.

To put it another way, I needed to find a witness. But apart from Monica and the man with the brown fender, there seemed to have been nobody except poor old Doug Gaulton in the house during those mysterious two hours of that Saturday morning.

The older I get, the more I am aware that people tend to treat old people as though they don't have good sense. And if you take the case of someone like Doug—why, folks think of him as the living dead. Because he can't talk or write or communicate in any way except by making that noise in his throat, people suppose he has no mind at all.

I had been wondering all along if he knew something that the rest of us didn't know. I could tell by his eyes and the way he would cry when I would talk about old times that he understood everything I said to him. If I could just think of some way he could tell *me* what he knew!

Many times when I leaned over his bed and took his hands in mine to talk to him, it seemed to me that he had a little movement in that left hand. Maybe he could tap something out—like Morse code. But Lord have mercy! Both of us would have to learn the code if we were going to talk like that.

There is braille for the blind and sign language for the deaf. But those things weren't going to be of any use to Doug and me.

Then I happened to think—Ouija!

There was such a craze for Ouija—oh, I don't remember how long ago. And I still had the board in a trunk in my attic.

You know what a Ouija board is. It is a board about twenty inches wide by about twenty-six inches long, and it has the alphabet painted on it in big letters. Then in one corner it has "yes" and in the opposite corner it has "no." There is a heart-shaped pointer called a planchette that rolls across the board.

It takes two people to work this thing. They put their hands on the planchette and ask the Ouija a question. Then the pointer rolls—all by itself, ha! ha!—it rolls by itself from one letter to another until it spells out the answer.

We used to have Ouija parties, and they were a lot of fun. The players were not supposed to push; so if you had a smart aleck answer you wanted the Ouija to spell out, you always accused your partner of shoving and then made the Ouija say whatever you wanted it to.

I just wondered if Doug would have enough movement in his left hand to push the pointer over that board. I thought it was worth a try.

I don't go up into my attic anymore. You see, I just have a disappearing stairway and it's very shaky. So when I need to put something up there, or get something that's already there, I call my little neighbor from next door. She is such a darling!

So I called her and told her where to find the Ouija. She had never seen one, and I had to explain it all to her after she had got it down for me. She had a fit about it—thought it was quaint—said she would borrow it sometime.

To get back to what I was telling—I took the Ouija board over to Doug's place. I explained to Mrs. Greene what I wanted.

"Oh," she said—she was so pleased—"I think he can do it. He does move that left hand. The doctor says it is involuntary, but I have seen Mr. Gaulton move that hand like he knew what he was doing. I always know he wants something when I see that hand move."

Anyhow, we thought we would try it out.

So Mrs. Greene worked the button that makes the bed come up the way it does, until Doug was almost sitting up. Then we put the board across his lap.

I said, "Doug, you know what this is. It's a Ouija board. Now, I am going to ask you some questions and I want you to push the pointer and spell out the answers."

He looked at me so steady. I knew he understood.

Mrs. Greene was on the other side of the bed, and she was about as interested in my little experiment as I was.

I put the planchette on the board and lifted poor old Doug's left hand and set it on the pointer.

"Now, here is my question," I said. "Do you know anything about the poison that killed Monica?"

I said it real slow and repeated it. Doug was looking at me just as steady as the Rock of Gibraltar. I knew he understood me.

Then that hand began to move very slowly, and the pointer traveled a jerky path toward the far left corner of the board.

"Do you mean 'yes'?"

The movement stopped.

"Isn't that wonderful!" Mrs. Greene said.

"Can you tell us anything?" I asked.

Doug's eyes went to the board. The movement of his

hand was painfully slow and—I guess "tentative" is the best word.

The pointer went to *M,* and Mrs. Greene grabbed a pencil and a little tablet that she had and took down the letters.

After the *M* came *E, A,* and *N.*

"Mean?" I asked. Doug looked straight into my eyes, then down at the board again.

He shoved the pointer to *T* and looked up at me as if to say that *T* was part of the word also.

So the word was *MEANT.*

We urged Doug to rest a little if it was too hard for him, but he went on.

The next word was easy. It was *FOR.*

Then Doug rested quite a while. I thought maybe we weren't going to get anything else.

The last word was *ME.*

MEANT FOR ME

"Meant for me!" That certainly threw another light on the matter. That explained why with all our investigation of the "murder" of Monica Gaulton we had been unable to find anything.

Yes, there were reasons why a good many people had wanted to get Monica out of the way. But if the message Doug had spelled out on the Ouija board was correct, Monica's death was an accident connected with a plan to murder Doug.

No sooner had this thought crossed my mind than a great doubt almost wiped it out. How did Doug know the cyanide was meant for him? Or did he just imagine it?

I truly believe that people in a helpless state—like Doug—must think a lot about death. Surely they must want release. But then again there is always a spark that holds on to life. Could Doug have been afraid for some time that Monica would poison him? And then I thought about the will he had made in favor of Monica. Maybe Doug regretted not leaving his money to his children—'specially if he thought Monica was going to murder him for the estate.

Perhaps I shouldn't take the message of the Ouija so seriously.

I said to Doug, very slowly and plain: "How do you know?"

As soon as I said it, I wished I hadn't. Such a wild look came into Doug's eyes, and he made that awful sound in his throat. If I had ever had any doubt that Doug understood what was said and done around him, that doubt would have been gone in an instant.

I said, "Doug, you must tell us."

There was more of that awful noise.

"Doug, we need to know."

His eyes fell once more to the Ouija board, and the feeble movement of the hand began the long trek to the far right corner.

NO

"He is not going to tell us," I said to Mrs. Greene.

Doug's eyes looked straight into mine. Was it my imagination that the expression was different—that it was almost a glare. There was no guttural sound from his throat. He had told us in effect that he would say no more.

I went home and did a lot of thinking. If the poison was intended for Doug, the person who was most to be suspected was Monica. But Monica was the one who died, and the thing was just as mysterious as it ever was. If the cyanide was meant by Monica or anyone else for Doug, something unexpected must have happened. The poison somehow had got into the flask—by accident? How could anybody be so careless with cyanide that the wrong person would be killed. And if the poison was intended for Doug and someone else came along and—I guess you would have to say "diverted" it to Monica—wouldn't we be back where we started, and wouldn't we have to ask who would want to murder Monica?

Well, it was just a worse puzzle than it had been before. I spent the whole day thinking about it, and my poor brain was so tired that I went to bed that night and slept like a log.

I don't know whether I did any thinking while I was asleep, but in the morning I knew I had to talk with Mrs. Greene again.

Now, I had disturbed Doug enough the day before. It was perfectly obvious that he did not want me to know who told him the poison was meant for him.

So when Mrs. Greene let me into the house, I said, "Honey, I'm not going up to Doug's room today; but you've got to tell me something."

"All right," she said.

"On that Saturday that Monica died, Olive Gifford saw a man get out of an old beat-up car—blue with one brown fender—and come in the back door here. Was that car here when you came to the house?"

"No. There wasn't any car at all."

"Did you ever see a car like that come up to this house?"

"No."

"I believe you said Monica—Mrs. Gaulton—had told you not to come in until ten o'clock. Had she ever done that before?"

"No, she hadn't."

"Did she give a reason?"

"No."

"Was she in the house when you came in?"

"Yes, I heard her in her room."

"Was there anybody else here when you came in?"

"No."

"Could Doug—Mr. Gaulton—have had a visitor before you came on duty?"

"You know," she said, "I have been thinking about that ever since you were here yesterday. Mr. Gaulton was upset when I came in that morning. I could tell. But I thought nothing of it. It is amazing how patient he is. You just wonder why he isn't cross all the time. I really think somebody might have been here."

"Do you have any notion who it could have been?"

"Well," she said, "the two most faithful visitors are that old black woman who used to work for him—and Nathan. Nathan just adores Mr. Gaulton!"

Nathan, you remember, is Bill and Jan's boy. And the old black woman is Lily Dabney. Years ago Lily was the cook for the Gaultons for I don't know how long, and Jackson—that was Lily's husband—was the chauffeur and handy man.

"And Nathan and Lily come in right often, do they?"

"Oh, yes. It is a rare day that Nathan doesn't come in to see his 'Big Dad'—on his way home from school or on Saturday morning. And the other one is here two or three times a week."

So the thing for me to do was to have a little talk with Lily.

She lives in a nice little house not far from Doug's. She was glad to see me, and her sweet old black face brought back so many memories. We just hugged each other.

I'll tell you one thing: there was no love lost between her and Monica. Lily knew Monica wasn't in the same class as Iris Gaulton.

Well, we talked a little about old times. Lily was getting along pretty well. I knew Jackson had been dead for a while, but she said her children were good to her. She has a granddaughter who is a schoolteacher and lives back of her. All of her folks were good people.

But to get to what she told me.

When she got to the house that day, she let herself in. It was about eight-fifteen. Monica had just got up and was in her robe. She was not at all happy to see Lily, but that didn't surprise Lily, because Monica never did like to see her.

The two of them were up there in Doug's room. When Lily realized that the nurse had not come in, she offered to stay with Doug until Mrs. Greene arrived. Monica didn't take to the idea and told Lily she would have to leave because she, Monica, was going to give Doug an enema.

Can you imagine Monica Taybrook giving Doug Gaulton an enema! Yes, I know: cats love water and horses have wings.

The car with the brown fender had not arrived when Lily left.

So I hadn't learned anything from Lily.

I learned a lot from Nathan. But I don't believe I am going to tell it just yet.

XXIV

Music Club Business

HELEN DELAPORTE

Our poor Music Club! When Harriet found the culprit of the DAR murder, it was written up in a book, as you know. We got 1,569 inches of newspaper publicity for our Old Orchard Fort Chapter, NSDAR. Not all of it was the kind we wanted. Nevertheless, we were given credit for it by National Headquarters, and they were rather proud of us in Washington.

But nobody was proud of what was going on in our Music Club. Tolah Stalker had a solid point about our notoriety. It wasn't pleasant to read about ourselves in the bold headlines of *The American Exposé*. But Tolah always makes things worse when she tries to make them better.

Which brings me to Ernestine Fuller and her threatened resignation from the club. That was something we absolutely could not let happen.

Ernestine is a very fine person and a valuable member of the club. She is a good teacher with about thirty piano students. I doubt that apart from the Music Club she has much social life; and to let her resign because of Tolah would be just too bad.

I had real empathy for Ernestine. She is timid; this was the first time she had been asked to take care of anything as big as the fashion show. It wasn't an easy assignment. Yet she did her best. If Monica Gaulton had only waited until after the show to sip her whiskey, everything would have been all right.

I don't even fault Ernestine's choice of Monica for mistress of ceremonies. It truly had brought a high degree of interest to the program, for everyone was eager to see Monica's performance.

And the proceeds from the tickets, which were sold on the basis of Ernestine's selection of Monica, were excellent.

How Tolah could associate Ernestine with the chain of events that had landed our Music Club on the pages of *The American Exposé*, I cannot imagine. I suppose there is something in the primitive psyche that attempts to transfer all mental pain elsewhere; and to drive Ernestine out of the club like the Scapegoat out of the camp of Israel may have appealed to Tolah as a healing action.

However, I was determined that Ernestine should be no scapegoat.

I talked to her very severely. I told her that she had no right to submit to the bullying of a person like Tolah Stalker—that the club needed and appreciated her and that she had no business resigning. In short, I told her to pull up her socks and fight back.

She cried and felt better. And before I had left her house, she had agreed to retract her resignation.

I didn't know what Tolah would think, but I didn't care.

XXV

The Horseshoe Nail

HARRIET GARDNER BUSHROW

There used to be something in my copybook about how a battle was lost "all for the want of a horseshoe nail." Goodness, it was such a long time ago when we used to have to write those things out in Spencerian script! Well, the point was that no matter how little a condition or event is, it influences things that are much more important.

In this case the "horseshoe nail"—that wasn't lost, and so the battle was won—is a combination of the condition of my hose and the work the city was doing on Division Street. You might add to that the weather on Wednesday, January 21.

That was the morning I realized that I must buy some new hose. Every time I buy new hose, I think surely these will last till I die. But so far it never has worked out that way.

It was not until four o'clock that I got to the mall to make my purchase. There had been sun that had melted much of the snow that fell the day before.

Naturally I drove out Division Street, the street that divides Borderville, Tennessee, from Borderville, Virginia. It is awkward sometimes living in a city that lies across a state line. And it is specially awkward when one side of a street is in one town and the opposite side is even in a different state.

Just then Borderville, Tennessee, had its side of Division

Street torn up to repair a water main; and coming back from the mall, I had to take a detour on Sycamore.

With the temperature around thirty-six degrees, the street was clear, though the snow along the sides was melting and running down the gutters. I was just thinking how slick the streets would be when it got really cold later on. Then what should I see but a blue car with one brown fender parked in front of a rooming house on the other side of Sycamore.

I pulled over to the curb and fished around in my pocketbook for my little notepad. At last I was going to get that man's license number and, no doubt, the address of the place where he lived as well.

I took down the address and started to get out of my car to walk over where I could see the license number. I had no more than set one foot on the ground when I looked up, and there was the man himself.

He recognized me right off. It's that gold color of my car that makes it stand out. He remembered me, never fear.

I looked at him, and he looked at me, and he was the meanest old thing I ever laid eyes on.

When he started over to my side of the street, I just pulled my foot back in the car, shut my door, and got the Buick going as fast as I could.

I hadn't gone more than a block when I saw in the mirror that he had turned his car around and was coming after me.

This time he was the one trying to find out about me—which I didn't like at all. I rounded corners and went every which way. I ran red lights, hoping the cops might see me, but they didn't.

In my running around and dodging, I turned the corner from Maple on to Seventeenth, where there is one of those car-wash places. I was far enough ahead of Mr. Brown Fender that he couldn't see me. So I drove into the car wash and hid in one of the stalls.

I could hear his car go by in the water that was running across the street. I just sat there about fifteen minutes until I thought he had had time to give up the chase. Then I drove on home.

Now, why the man was on Sycamore Street instead of at the adult book store, I don't know. Maybe he had lost his job out there. Or maybe his hours had changed. But none of that matters.

The point is that I got home about five-thirty.

Wednesday night is Church Night Supper at my church. So I had thirty minutes to get ready and get over there.

The Bible Study following the supper would last until about eight-thirty, and by that time the streets would be slick, not to mention my driveway, which would be a regular sheet of ice.

I don't know whether you get as many catalogs as I do. I just love them. I sit in my room by a window where I can get a good light and look at all the things I don't need and don't want. But every once in a while I see something that looks pretty good.

That's how I got my "Neet Kleets." I saw them in one of those catalogs.

These Neet Kleets are plates of metal with rough things on the bottom like on a carrot grater. Then there are straps that you buckle over your overshoes so that you don't have to be at all afraid of walking on ice.

With my cane and these Neet Kleets I can just go anywhere in bad weather, and I don't have to be isolated or stay in the house.

I freshened up a bit and got my Neet Kleets and took my Bible, and off I went.

Dr. McDavit, our fine minister, is such a wonderful Bible teacher and so well known in the denomination that I wouldn't miss one of his lessons for anything.

By the time the meeting was over, sure enough, all the

water from the snow had frozen, and on the streets there were patches of ice everywhere.

I drove as carefully as I could—I have radial tires—and when I got to my drive, just as I had thought, it was slick as a whistle. But I got the car into the garage without any trouble and started to walk toward the house with my Neet Kleets and Grandfather Gardner's gold-handled cane, when suddenly I looked up and caught my breath.

It was that man!

He came out of the shadow and was beside me before I knew it. He had a gun.

He said, "All right, sister. . . ."

Like sleight of hand, it was so quick, I reversed Grandfather Gardner's cane and caught that fellow's ankle with it. With just a little pull, his feet flew out from under him, and his gun went slithering in one direction while he went in the other. Much to his surprise he found himself lying on the ground.

I have no idea how I had the presence of mind to do all that so quickly. It gives me the shivers to think back on it.

There's no point in talking about what might have happened, because what actually happened was just perfect.

You should have seen that fellow trying to get up—legs and arms going in all directions. Meanwhile I had picked up his pistol and had it pointed right at him.

I guess I should have kept him there and held him until the police came, but I didn't see how I could.

Instead I said, "Get yourself out of here, mister, before I pull this trigger."

He went slipping and sliding down that driveway as fast he could, and pretty soon I heard a car start up.

I went into the house without even taking off my Neet Kleets and called the police. I gave them the man's address and told them that he had attacked me with a deadly weapon and if they would get to his place soon enough, they could arrest him. I said I would get there as quick as I could and tell them as much as I knew about that fellow.

They did just what I asked—went out to his place on Sycamore and arrived a minute or so after he got there.

Now. I am going to break off my story and insert what the newspaper said the next morning. Of course what it said wasn't quite true, but it was interesting to read.

RESIDENT ATTACKED BY

GAULTON DEATH SUSPECT

Mrs. L. Q. C. Lamar Bushrow, 90, of Borderville, Tenn., was accosted at her residence, 521 Powell Street, at 9:00 P.M. on Wednesday by Wesley D. Welch. The attack was made with a .38-caliber Smith and Wesson as Bushrow returned home from a service at Borderville's First Presbyterian Church.

Through the courageous action of the elderly victim, the accused attacker was apprehended at his residence at 1117 Sycamore Street some thirty minutes after he was routed from the scene of the attack.

"I knocked him down and took his gun away from him," Bushrow stated with a twinkle in her eye. Enlarging upon her statement, she explained that she gained possession of the accused's weapon when he slipped and fell on the ice in her driveway.

"I think you will find that this man had something to do with the death of Monica Gaulton," Bushrow observed. "You will just have to wait and see," she added.

Police were searching the residence of the accused and had no further comment for the *Ban-ner-Democrat* at press time.

All right, that is what the paper printed on Thursday, but here is what really happened.

When I got to that house on Sycamore, the police were already there—two patrol cars of them. They had surrounded the house, and the man was inside refusing to come out.

The police had their guns ready in case the man might start one of those shootouts we hear so much about. Fat chance, because I had the man's pistol right with me!

Anyhow, they had to wait until they could get a search warrant, and I had to accuse the fellow before they could get that. When I told them what I knew about the man, they were eager to interrogate the suspect. By ten o'clock the warrant had arrived and they had arrested my Mr. Brown Fender.

Upon searching the house, they were surprised to find a printing press in the basement and some engraving plates. There were bundles of paper and containers of different inks, and I don't know what-all. And—*counterfeit hundred-dollar bills!*

No, the bills weren't very convincing. Even I could tell there was something wrong. One of the policemen—a nice young man named Raymond Edwards—said he didn't think these bills would pass. He said our government has come out with a way of putting a nylon thread into the paper on which hundred-dollar bills are printed.

Of course I don't handle many hundred-dollar bills, but this Raymond Edwards, who seemed to know a lot about it, said that the thread is not visible unless the bill is held up to the light.

Then he showed me one of the counterfeit bills. It had the

thread in it, all right; but it was very evident without holding the paper to the light—too evident, don't you see.

So you might say that the counterfeiter hadn't yet come up with the right paper to make the counterfeit satisfactory.

I held one of those bills in my hand and just looked at it. That piece of paper explained a lot. Nowadays a counterfeit bill will have to be on good counterfeit paper. Now, just think. This fellow with the brown fender had a job with Cooksport Printing and Engraving, didn't he? So that's how he got the use of the equipment he needed. And remember that when I was sitting in my car across the highway from that adult book store, the man got upset when I said I was watching the paper factory for the anti-pollution people. Maybe he had somebody over there working on the paper he had to have to make hundred-dollar bills. And, of course, he would have to bribe any number of people to keep them from reporting him.

I told the police all about it, and they were very interested. Our officers would have to notify the Treasury Department because counterfeiting and all that is a federal offense.

I tell you it was quite a night. I didn't get home until almost two o'clock, and that's hard on an old lady.

The next morning the District Attorney called me about ten and asked me to come to his office at two.

He is a very nice man—name is Malcolm Lindsay. He had me sit in a comfortable chair and talk into his tape recorder.

He said, "Just tell me what you know about Monica Gaulton's death."

Now I am going to have to stop my story and go back again.

I never could tell a story straight. The way I did it used to make Lamar so mad, he would say, "Harriet, if you would just think what you are going to say before you start out, you could say it in half the time." And I would say, "Who says I want to tell it in half the time?"

So what I am going to tell next happened a week before, and I couldn't tell it then because it would have given the whole thing away.

XXVI

Honest Confession

HARRIET GARDNER BUSHROW

After that Ouija board told us that the cyanide in Monica's drink was really meant for Doug, I knew that there was somebody who didn't want Monica to become a widow just yet, and that was the person, most likely, who had turned the tables on her. But who was it?

It stood to reason that whoever changed the way things happened must have come into the Gaulton house on that Saturday morning between eight and ten. And the only two people who were regular visitors and would come and go without making themselves known to Monica would have to be Lily and Nathan..

Now I have already told you how I questioned Lily and was satisfied that she did not know anything that would help me. So that left Nathan.

Well, I would have to get "parental permission" to question that boy about something that came so close to the very nerve of the family; but, as you know, Janet had been helpful in this business, and the family was getting pretty tired of the whole mess. So Janet said, sure, I could ask Nathan anything I wanted to, but please be careful about it because she didn't want him any more upset than he already was.

Jan and Bill live in a two-story colonial frame house on Maple Street, about a block and a half from Doug's place.

Jan is a very practical young woman—has plain, good taste, modern furniture, everything comfortable for family living. She has her head screwed on right.

Jan and Nathan were waiting for me when I got to the house. As I eased myself down into one of Jan's big, comfortable chairs, there didn't seem to be a very convenient place to lean my cane.

I said to Nathan, "Young man, I wonder if you wouldn't just set my cane over there against the wall somewhere."

I had noticed already that that child's eyes were on that gold handle of my cane. "Do you like my cane?" I asked. He didn't say anything, but I could tell he was just as interested in that gold handle as he could be. So I told him about it.

"That cane was given to my grandfather Gardner. He lived down in Georgia and was a judge. And that cane was presented to him when he retired." Then I showed him the inscription on the handle.

"Is that real gold?"

Well, of course that is what anybody would want to know and only a child would ask.

"Yes, it is," I said. "And that gold was mined in Georgia."

He looked at me in surprise.

"Yes, we had a gold rush in Dahlonega, Georgia, long before anybody even thought of California or Alaska or any of those places."

Nathan seemed to be fascinated.

"I tell you what," I said, "I'll put this cane in my will for you, if you would like to have it."

You see, I have no family left and I have all this stuff that means a lot to me. And I just thought, the gold handle is probably worth a lot now, and when I am gone it will be melted up and that will be the end of it. But if I leave it to this child, he will treasure it and tell his children, "An old lady gave me this cane with a handle of gold mined in Georgia." And wouldn't that have pleased Grandfather Gardner!

Janet prompted the child to thank me properly. But I could see the thanks in his face.

So we were on the same wavelength now.

"Nathan, I believe you visit your grandfather right often," I began.

He nodded. It isn't easy for an eleven-year-old to carry on a conversation with a ninety-year-old woman that he doesn't know very well, and, besides, I could tell that I was edging onto a sensitive subject.

"I think that's wonderful," I continued. "It means a lot to your grandfather."

Nathan looked embarrassed—or was he nervous?

"Did your mother tell you that I had a conversation with your grandfather?"

"With a Ouija board," he replied.

"And did she tell you what a Ouija board is?"

She had told him about the Ouija board, but I judged that she had not told Nathan what it was I had learned from the Ouija. And that was good, because I had the advantage of surprise.

"Well, your grandfather says the poison that killed that poor woman was intended for him. What do you think about that?"

His eyes got larger and very apprehensive.

"Now you were there that morning, weren't you?"

The boy didn't say anything.

His mother said, "Tell Mrs. Bushrow, Nathan. Tell her whether you were at Big Dad's the morning Monica died."

"Don't be afraid," I said. "Just tell the truth. Nobody will say you are to blame if you did the right thing. You did do the right thing, didn't you?"

I thought the child was going to cry. I don't care how

sophisticated young folks are nowadays with television and Nintendo or whatever they call it, eleven years old is still childhood. We put children in adult situations awfully early today. But there is nothing new about that. Think of what the children in pioneer days had to do. But a child of eleven—what a strain he must have gone through! Well I must get on with my story.

"Yes, ma'am."

He is a very polite child.

"Well, then," I went on, "just tell us what happened."

Miss Birmingham, Nathan's fifth-grade teacher, had assigned him a book report on *A Tale of Two Cities*. Nathan had put off reading the assignment and put it off until the report was almost due. When he went to the school library to get the book on the Friday before Monica's death, *A Tale of Two Cities* had been checked out.

What was he to do?

If you will look at the floor plan of Doug Gaulton's house, you will see that there is a library just off the living room and that there is a door from the library to the breakfast room. And then there is a door to the back hall and a door from the back hall to the kitchen.

You must remember that Monica wasn't very hospitable to Doug's family and really didn't care to have them coming into the house all the time—especially Nathan. And that was a foolish attitude, because it meant that Nathan was all the more likely to sneak into the house without her knowing it.

That is exactly what he did that Saturday morning. He went first into the library to look for his book. Iris always encouraged her children to read. And so there was one corner of the library where the children's books were kept. Since there had been three boys in the family, there was a collection of the Rover Boys and other books that boys read back then and probably would still like now if they could get their hands on them.

Well, Nathan was in that corner quietly looking into those books—at the pictures and so on—when Monica and a man came into the breakfast room and began talking.

"It won't be hard to do. I've got the stuff right here," the man said. Nathan was standing behind the open library door, where he could look through the crack and see nearly everything. Monica and the man were at the breakfast room table. The man had his back toward the door between the breakfast room and the library, and Monica was seated so that she was not looking in Nathan's direction. The conversation must have gone something like this:

"I don't want to do this," Monica would have said.

"It is cyanide. He will never know it happened. Once you get it in him, he will go out like a light."

"You are asking me to murder him."

"What the hell! He's three-quarters dead already. Think of it as mercy killing."

"What if there is an autopsy."

"There won't be any autopsy. You are the widow. You can say you don't want one. Besides, in his shape he could shove off just any day now on his own."

"Then why not wait for that?"

"I need the money now. It will take enough time to get our hands on it after he is gone without having to wait around for the old goat to kick off."

"I don't like to do this."

"You don't *like!* You went through three hundred thousand of my money"—Nathan reported that the man said 'three million,' but we found out later that it was three hundred thousand—"You lost three hundred thousand of my money and you don't *like* something! Just remember what I can do to you if you don't do this for me."

"You wouldn't. You know what *I* could do to you."

"But you know what you are *going* to do. You are going to do just what I tell you."

"How do I do it?"

"You put it in that muck you feed him."

It seemed they talked on something like that for a while, and all the time Nathan was watching and listening.

Finally Monica said, "I haven't had my breakfast. I'll fix you some eggs," and they went into the kitchen.

That gave Nathan his chance. He sneaked into the breakfast room—you know all the children and half the adult population wear those athletic shoes that just don't make any noise at all.

There on the table was a little brown bottle with a cork in the top. In it was what looked like a white powder. Nathan knew right away that it was the poison that the man and Monica were planning to put into Doug's food, and Nathan had to get rid of it.

But how?

The best way would be to wash it down the sink. But Monica and the man were in the kitchen. And besides, if either of them looked toward the door, there was the little brown bottle on the breakfast table right where they could see it.

Nathan had to move in a hurry.

As he looked around, that flask on the shelf in the built-in cabinet caught his eye. It would take only a second to pour the powder into the flask. Whether the child thought of it or not, Doug was never going to drink out of that thing again.

The flask was the only way to get rid of the poison both quietly and quickly. So very carefully, he poured the white powder into the flask, put the top back on it, and replaced the flask on the shelf.

But what about the empty bottle?

On the breakfast room table was the sugar bowl.

Carefully Nathan spooned sugar into the brown bottle. He corked it and put it back exactly where the man had left it.

After Nathan had told his story, he looked as if he expected some dreadful punishment. I said, "Young man, you did exactly the right thing."

"But—Monica is dead."

The poor child must have worried about that for months!

"Come over here," I said. "I want to hold your hands while I tell you something."

I took his hands in mine and looked into his eyes. "You didn't kill Monica. She put the whiskey in that flask when she had no business to do it. You did the only thing you could do, and you are not responsible for anything other people do."

He didn't say anything.

I squeezed his hands and said, "Now promise me that you won't fret about this anymore."

A look of relief dawned slowly across his face and turned into a smile. I'll say this: the Gaultons breed true to form.

So there it was. That child never had the slightest notion that the cyanide he had put into the flask was going to kill Monica.

Of course not.

And that meant that Monica hadn't been murdered at all.

But to go on with the story. As soon as Nathan had replaced the bottle on the table, he went back through the library and the living room to the front stairs. He ran up to his grandfather's room and told him that Monica and a man were trying to poison him.

Then he heard Monica come up the stairs. He was afraid she would find him in Doug's room, but at the head of the stairs she turned into her own room. Pretty soon he heard the shower running in her bathroom.

That gave Nathan his chance. He went downstairs and

was going to pour out the cyanide into the kitchen sink. But to his dismay, when he got into the breakfast room, the flask was gone. Monica or the man had taken it.

There was a real dilemma for anybody. But it must have been awful for a child. It looked as though somebody was going to be poisoned by drinking out of that flask. Would it be Monica? Or would it be the man? What was Nathan to do? Go tell Monica? That would let the cat out of the bag for sure. He knew for certain that Monica was somebody he ought to be afraid of, and what he had just heard made it so much worse.

What would you do in a case like that?

Well, Nathan just went home; and from that day until he told the story to me and his mother, he didn't say anything about Monica, the man, or the poison.

XXVII

I Explain to the D.A.

HARRIET GARDNER BUSHROW

Now we will go back to where I was sitting in the District Attorney's office. He asked me to tell what I knew about Monica Gaulton's death. And I told him just what I told you in the last chapter.

Then I told him what Olive Gifford had said about those New Age children dancing around in the moonlight and about the old car with one brown fender, and how I just happened to think of saying I was watching the paper factory to help the environment people, and how I saw now that there must have been somebody connected with that factory who was helping the man—incidentally his real name turned out to be Kimler, Warren David Kimler—somebody who had been trying to make that paper with the nylon thread in it.

Mr. Lindsay made a note of it, but said if I was right about that, the man would probably be gone already but they would find him.

Mr. Lindsay was very complimentary to me for what I had done. He also told me that they had found out that Kimler had escaped from federal prison, where he was supposed to be doing twenty years on a counterfeiting conviction.

"I guess you have his record," I said.

"Well, no," he answered. "That part of it doesn't come under our jurisdiction. Counterfeiting is a federal offense. No, we don't have the record yet. We'll get it, though," he replied. "Is there something in the record you want to know?"

I told him there were two things I wanted. He said he would get the information for me.

I went home and tried to fit everything together in my mind. As the picture formed, I began to feel sorry for Monica Taybrook.

Monica had been such a pretty little thing. And her sweet mother had been just so full of love and ambition for her one lone chick. Mosene Taybrook, working away at that sewing machine, what did all her effort come to?

There is a moral around here somewhere, but I can't seem to lay my finger on it. There are so many things in this world that we don't understand!

XXVIII

WOMAN FINGERS COUNTERFEITER

Warren David Kimler of 2117 Sycamore, whose name was erroneously reported in yesterday's *Borderville Banner-Democrat* as Wesley D. Welch, has been identified as an escapee from Allentown Federal Prison in Pennsylvania, where he had been serving time for counterfeiting.

Kimler, who was arrested late Wednesday and charged with having made an attack with a dangerous weapon on Mrs. L. Q. C. Lamar Bushrow of 521 Powell Street, Borderville, Tenn., is expected to be taken into federal custody sometime today.

Asked if she was surprised that her attacker was also a counterfeiter, Bushrow replied, "Not at all. I had been watching that young man for weeks. He was obviously no good."

Kimler had been living in the Borderville area for the past year and was employed by the XXX Adult Book Store and by Cooksport Printing and Engraving.

The *Banner-Democrat* was informed that certain evidence was found in the basement of Kimler's residence, but the nature of the evidence was not revealed.

XXIX

A Judgment of Solomon

HARRIET GARDNER BUSHROW

That story came out in the Friday paper. I had no more than got through reading it when the phone rang, and it was the young woman at the District Attorney's office wanting me to go down there and talk to Mr. Lindsay again. I got to the courthouse just as the clock was striking ten. Mr. Lindsay seated me in the same leather chair where I had sat before, and was very cordial.

"Mrs. Bushrow," he began, "we got the information you asked for from his record."

"And he was married to her?"

"Yes, married to Monica Joy Taybrook in the Borough of Brooklyn on June 27, 1962."

"And was there a divorce?"

"There is no record of it."

"So that was the hold he had over her. And because he was an escaped convict, she had a hold over him."

"Yes. Kimler tells us he had hidden away over $300,000. Upon his escape from Allentown, he discovered that Monica had found his trove and squandered it. Newer techniques to prevent counterfeiting have made counterfeiting that much more expensive for the counterfeiter. Having found Monica married bigamously to a wealthy and moribund invalid, Kimler was demanding his $300,000, part of which, at least, he needed because he was working on a method of counterfeiting that could not be detected."

With this bit of information the mystery was completely explained.

After Monica got money from Conrad and Norman Gaulton so she could go away and have the baby that never was, she went to New York for her "career." Considerably later, she met and married my man with one brown fender.

After Kimler was convicted, Monica found his hoard of real money and spent it as she so well knew how to do. Then there was Las Vegas, which for her had the double attraction of offering employment and facilities for gambling.

When she had been cleaned out there, she stole the car from the rental people and came back to Borderville to sponge off of her old high-school chum, Edna Finch. Poor Doug Gaulton fell into her web, and she had visions of wealth beyond anything she had ever dreamed. It was inconvenient to have to put up with a helpless invalid who persisted in living in spite of all expectation. But that was only a temporary difficulty, with which she could deal, since her ultimate success was in sight.

But unexpectedly, out of the past came her legal husband demanding money and more money. Kimler himself could manage the engraving for his counterfeiting endeavor. But making the paper to duplicate what the government is now using was quite another proposition. This was something he could not do himself. He would have to corrupt someone who had expertise of the highest kind in order to have a supply of satisfactory paper. And no doubt there would be others whose silence would have to be bought. I can't imagine that an activity of that sort would be easily hidden in a modern paper factory.

Where there is bribery there is bound to be a kind of mutual blackmail involved. No doubt those who had been bribed by Kimler demanded more and more from him.

And so Kimler demanded more and more from Monica.

Bill Gaulton had clamped down so much on her money supply that she had to scramble to scrape up whatever cash she could lay her hands on. That was why she sold the living room furniture. That was why she gambled. That was why she milked those poor New Age young people for every cent she could get.

But none of it satisfied Kimler, and finally he demanded Douglass Gaulton's death.

But to get back to my conversation with Mr. Lindsay—

"Well," I said, "this man did not murder Douglass Gaulton, but he wanted to. I suppose there is some way he can be charged with that."

"No," Mr. Lindsay replied, "I don't think that would be a good idea."

"Surely you are not going to let him get away with a thing like this!" I was shocked at the very thought.

"The consequences outweigh the satisfaction of the law."

I didn't understand, and he must have seen it in my facial expression.

"Mrs. Bushrow," he explained, "all our evidence comes from an eleven-year-old boy. I have talked to Nathan, and I believe him. But imagine putting that boy on the witness stand. Any lawyer at all could make mincemeat of his testimony.

"In the first place Nathan is a minor. How much of his testimony was the work of an imagination overheated by the sensational death of Mrs. Gaulton and the subsequent interrogation of his great-uncles, his great-aunt, his father and mother, not to mention the nurses that took care of his great-grandfather?

"In the second place, he is an heir to the estate according to the earlier will of Douglass Gaulton. The making of the subsequent will invalidates the prior instrument, true enough, but for purposes of the defense lawyer that would make little difference. The defense could eat that boy alive.

"I know it is not a good thing to bully a child before a jury. But look at it through the eyes of the defense. It wouldn't be the child who concocted the story. It would be the greedy, corrupt, unspeakable Gaulton family who would be sacrificing this innocent lamb to free themselves from suspicion of murder.

"In the end we could probably make the charge of conspiracy to commit a crime stick, but I don't want to put that kid through the kind of thing that could happen.

"And don't forget, *The American Exposé* and all the other scandal sheets will be on to it."

I had to admit that everything Mr. Lindsay said was true. And Nathan is such a nice boy. Surely it was enough that he had saved Doug's life, what there is of it, and had had to keep all that stuff secret for months. Just think! The police were accusing everybody in his family except him, and after all he was the one who put the cyanide into the flask from which Monica drank and died. Think what that must have meant to him—wondering whether the police would blame him for the murder. Would they put him in jail? Would they send him to the chair? And if he didn't tell, would they send another of the Gaultons—maybe his father or mother—to the chair?

"You are right," I said, although I was a little disappointed. "Monica is dead, and this Kimler will go back to prison. Doug can't live more than a year or so at the most. I guess it is all to the good just to let the matter rest."

"Oh, we will prosecute Kimler for his attack on you," Mr. Lindsay said.

Yes, there was that.

I went on home—not exactly satisfied in my mind. There was this other thing that bothered me. All that inquisition of the Gaulton family. The whole town knew about the charges. All over town there were rumors about Doug's latest will and his former will.

And there would be doubts in people's minds about this whole thing—Did Norman do it? Did Conrad do it? and so on. That family would never get out from under public suspicion unless the truth came out.

So after about an hour, I called Mr. Lindsay and asked him if it would be all right if we made a book out of the sensational Music Club mystery the way we had made a book out of *The Famous DAR Murder Mystery* and *The Rotary Club Murder Mystery*. There wouldn't be any cross-examination of Nathan Gaulton, and the whole thing would be explained and nobody could blame the Gaultons at all for anything.

Yes, he said, he thought that would be all right if it was all right with the Gaulton family.

When I explained to them why the District Attorney did not wish to bring conspiracy charges against Kimler and why the truth must be told, they agreed.

Well, I said last time that I would never write anything like a book again unless they gave me a secretary.

And do you know what? That sweet Bill Gaulton brought a tape recorder to my house and showed me how to use it. So I just talked into it—oh, I'm good at talking—and then his secretary typed it up.

And then, of course, Vera McKendry and that darling Helen Delaporte and all the rest—well they contributed their parts.

So I think everything is explained now.

There is one more observation I want to make: I always knew that money was at the bottom of this mystery, but it was a great surprise to discover that *counterfeit* money was at the root of it. Then you might say that Monica and her career were counterfeit, too. What with her counterfeit pregnancy and her counterfeit marriage, you might say she ed a counterfeit life. And to think, she was in my Sunday School class all those years and years ago.

Incidentally, Tolah's piano student received a four-year applied music scholarship. The girl is just tickled to death and has given up the idea of being a vet. She will be going to Oberlin for a degree in music.

And, oh yes! There is one other pleasant note to bring this story to a close. You remember how Virginia Pettitoe went to Gatlinburg with that Mr. Bruster. Well, they are engaged and are going to get married next fall.